AMERICA'S
BETRAYAL

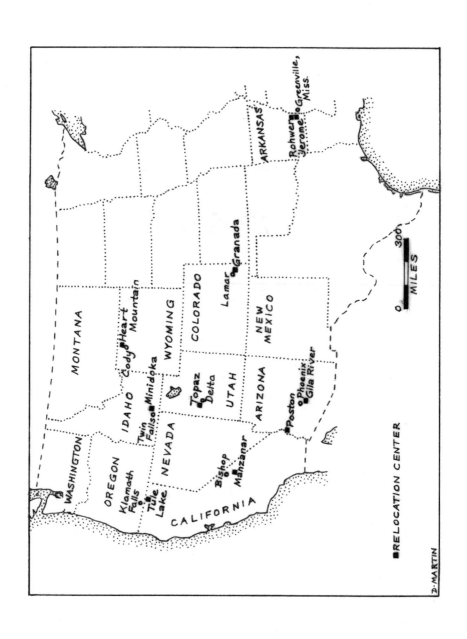

WASHINGTON

OREGON

Klamath
Falls

Tule
Lake

CALIFORNIA

Bishop

Manzanar

NEVADA

IDAHO

Twin
Falls

Minidoka

Cody

Heart
Mountain

WYOMING

MONTANA

Topaz

Delta

UTAH

COLORADO

Lamar

Granada

ARIZONA

Poston

Phoenix

Gila River

NEW
MEXICO

ARKANSAS

Rohwer

Jerome

Greenville,
Miss.

0   300

MILES

■ RELOCATION CENTER

D. MARTIN

AMERICA'S BETRAYAL

Jodi Icenoggle

WHITE MANE KIDS
SHIPPENSBURG, PENNSYLVANIA

This book is a work of fiction. Names, characters, places, and incidents either are products of the author's imagination or are used fictitiously. Any resemblance to actual events or locales or persons, living or dead, is entirely coincidential.

This White Mane Books publication
was printed by
Beidel Printing House, Inc.
63 West Burd Street
Shippensburg, PA 17257-0708 USA

The acid-free paper used in this book meets the guidelines for permanence and durability of the Committee on Production Guidelines for Book Longevity of the Council on Library Resources.

For a complete list of available publications
please write
White Mane Books
Division of White Mane Publishing Company, Inc.
P.O. Box 708
Shippensburg, PA 17257-0708 USA

Library of Congress Cataloging-in-Publication Data

Icenoggle, Jodi, 1967-
    America's betrayal / Jodi Icenoggle.
        p. cm.
    Includes bibliographical references.
    Summary: The United States' entry into World War II has devastating effects on a
Japanese American family, especially sixteen-year-old Margaret, whose first love is drafted.
    ISBN 1-57249-252-X
    1. Japanese Americans--Evacuation and relocation, 1942-1945--Juvenile fiction. [1.
Japanese Americans--Evacuation and relocation, 1942-1945--Fiction. 2. World War
1939-1945--United States--Fiction.] I. Title.

PZ7.I152 Am 2001
[Fic]--dc21

                                                          2001026814

For Grammie Moto,
With loving thanks for sharing your stories.
Without you, I would have remained ignorant
of this ugly chapter in our nation's history.
You're an inspiration and a treasure!

—Jodi

Contents

Contents

PREFACE

When I was twenty-three, I met an incredible woman who changed my view of our country and its history. She shared her family's stories of life before Pearl Harbor and after. Her parents had immigrated to America, started a family and raised ten children, all of whom were American citizens by birth. They enjoyed a better life than they would have in Japan. None of the children knew anything about Japan. Yet, they were forced to leave the only home they had ever known simply because of their appearance. They escaped California; others they knew were not so fortunate. Some friends were transported to relocation centers. Translation: internment.

After hearing her stories and learning more about the internment of Japanese Americans, I realized that America, a country built on freedom and equality, had deliberately imprisoned many of its citizens. I was appalled. I was outraged. I was determined to do something. This book was written in remembrance of those who suffered the indignities of internment. It is intended to honor those whose lives were forever disrupted by the forced evacuation of the West Coast and those who lived in the camps. It also was written in hope that our great country never repeats this horror. It is imperative we as a nation remember what happened to the Japanese Americans so we never dishonor our citizens again. Although this topic is difficult to discuss, its time has come.

ACKNOWLEDGMENTS

I wish to gratefully acknowledge and thank those who laid the groundwork—numerous authors and historians who fought popular opinion and insisted this subject be addressed. This is a work of fiction, based on facts. Extensive research was done to insure the accuracy of the facts presented within the story's context. President Roosevelt's actual words are not used within the book, but his speeches were consulted to maintain the tone and intent of his words. Valle Verde, California, is a fictional community, and the characters in this book are fictional people, to represent countless coastal communities which were affected by the evacuation. It is unintentional that any character represent any real person, living or deceased.

I also wish to thank the ladies of my critique group. I could never have accomplished this without all your comments and encouragement. Who's next?

And finally, to Bryan and my boys: Thank you for the support, the faith, and the prodding. You share me with the computer every day and let me pursue my dream of being a writer. I love you all.

CHAPTER 1
Sweet Sixteen

"It's a glorious day for Margaret's party, Mrs. Yamaguchi." Nancy breezed through the back door and planted a kiss on my mom's cheek.

I yanked Nancy down the stairs. Trixie, our cocker spaniel, trailed at our heels.

"You are *so* in like Flynn, Margaret," Nancy said excitedly. "John Wilson thinks you're a knockout!"

I tossed Nancy a bag of balloons. "He's so dreamy." I was excited about my first boy/girl party. "My parents won't let me date until I'm sixteen, but John and I have walked to school and eaten lunch together."

"With your brother Robert!" Nancy squealed.

"John and Robert have been friends forever. I've always tagged along." I smoothed streamers and taped them above the doorway as Trixie lay down. "Now, it's just different between John and me."

"Isn't it weird to like one of your brother's friends?" Nancy wrinkled her nose. "Even if it is John Wilson."

"It's a kick. If Robert didn't know John, my parents would be sore about me liking a senior."

1

"Margaret Yamaguchi, quit acting like it's no big deal. John's the hunk of heartbreak!" Nancy pinched me lightly. "He's captain of the football team. And the basketball team."

I rubbed my arm. "I'd like to hold his hand."

"He's so swoony, every deb in school wants to hold his hand."

"It does seem like a dream." I spotted my little brother on the stairs.

"Mother, make him stay upstairs!" I threw an empty box at Timmy. "It must be super to be an only child."

"Sometimes I wish I had brothers and sisters," Nancy admitted. "Especially an older brother with dreamy friends."

Despite Timmy, I laughed and thought about my family. My mother and father immigrated to America twenty-five years ago. My siblings and I were born here in Valle Verde, California. Robert was a senior in high school and planned on attending Stanford next fall. My older sister Barbara was married to Howard, and they lived nearby. My other brother was the pesky Timmy. He was always making my life icky. He spied on me, snitched on me, and set traps in my room. He drove me buggy!

"Nancy, who do you like?" I asked.

"He doesn't know I exist," Nancy said.

"Who?"

"I can't say." Nancy jumped up and tied balloons with ribbons.

"All the boys at school flirt with you," I teased.

"Not HIM."

"I wish I could talk to boys like you do," I admitted. "I get so nervous."

"I may flirt, but guys notice you."

"I'm too shy," I argued. "No one notices me."

"John did."

When we finished decorating, we dolled up for the party. We each wore a new princess dress, mine pink and Nancy's light green.

"I wish my parents would let me cut my hair." Nancy curled her fingers through mine. It was cut into a shoulder length bob, with bangs. "It's so swell. And you don't even have to tweeze your eyebrows." Nancy sighed.

My cousin Dorothy was the first guest. "Happy Birthday, Margaret," she said as we hugged. Dorothy and I were the same age, but she was a hip cheerleader and had been dating for a year.

"Don't you look cute, Nancy!" Dorothy cooed. "Both of you are just adorable." She hung her coat in the closet.

Nancy whispered, "Your cousin's a high hat."

"I think she's a knockout!" I whispered back. "Behave your-self, Nancy Sato."

"Just wait 'til she finds out John likes you." Nancy giggled and winked.

"Go on downstairs, Dot," I said as more guests showed up. "Barbara and Howard are chaperones."

John arrived next. Being so near to him made me feel all woozy.

"For you." John handed me a wrist corsage.

"Orchids are my favorite."

"That's what I was told," John said, looking embarrassed.

"Thank you." I slipped it on and led John to the basement on wobbly knees.

About twenty kids—mostly sophomores—filled the base-ment. I hoped I had invited the person Nancy liked, but she lingered around Robert.

"Hi, devil," Dorothy purred to John, swiveling her hips as she strutted toward him.

"Hubba, hubba, Dot." John whistled.

"Saving your dances for me?"

"I'm already taken by the birthday girl." He put his arm around my shoulders. "Care to cut a rug?" he asked me softly.

I concentrated on my feet, hoping I wouldn't stomp on his. One song ended and another began. "This is my favorite," I said. "It's luscious."

"What's the name of this one?"

" 'In the Mood.' "

"Glenn Miller's smooth."

Everyone danced and ate and laughed, but I hardly noticed anyone but John.

"Time to open presents!" Nancy shouted about nine o'clock.

I wanted to melt into the floor, and I knew my face was purple. But I smiled and stood by Nancy, who handed me packages. The first gift was from Elizabeth Parks who had moved from Michigan the previous summer.

"Thank you for the divine journal, Elizabeth."

"You're such a talented writer, Margaret."

"That's why she's on the *VV Sentinel*," said Daniel Rogers. "We're both going to be professional writers!"

Working on the school paper, the *VV Sentinel*, I became braver and more confident. Except around my family, I was painfully shy. If more than two or three friends gathered, I clammed up. But when I wrote, I was free.

"*For Whom the Bell Tolls* by Hemingway," I said.

My friends made my sweet-sixteen wonderful, with books by my favorite authors—John Steinbeck, F. Scott Fitzgerald, Virginia Wolf, records of Glenn Miller, Tommy Dorsey and Count Basie, and a hat pin from Robert.

"The one from the boutique!" I hugged my brother.

The last gift I opened was John's. I blushed as I unwrapped it. "What a beautiful satin ribbon."

Just before eleven o'clock, John took my hand and led me near the stairs. "I didn't want to do this in front of everybody." He fumbled in his jacket pocket and placed a small box in my hand. The lovely paper fell away.

Could he hear my heart pounding? My hands shaking, I lifted the lid. A pearl stickpin glinted. "It's beautiful." I stared at John, stunned.

"*You're* beautiful." He looked nervous. "Try it on."

"What will my parents say?"

"What if you have this?" John placed a gold chain around my neck. My mouth dropped open—his class ring hung from it. "Would you be my steady girl?"

I fingered the heavy ring. The room seemed too small. John leaned over and kissed me on the cheek. The party disappeared for a moment. I sensed a small body at the top of the stairs. My head swung around.

"Timmy," I hissed. "Beat it!" I charged toward my little brother.

"I saw you kissing!" Timmy cried gleefully as he ran off.

My cheeks were hot. Timmy had invaded my first kiss.

"Will you wear it?" John asked, pulling my thoughts back to the party.

I cradled the pin. "I love pearls."

"Doesn't Margaret mean pearl in Japanese?"

My eyes widened. "How did you know?"

"Sometimes it's good to have spies." He took my hand and led me back to the party. Nancy's eyes got huge. She dragged me over to the record player.

"Oolie droolie, Margaret!"

I couldn't stop giggling. "He asked me to be his steady girl." I hinged a glance at John. He and Robert were talking in the corner. Robert clapped John's shoulder.

"That's the cat's meow!" Nancy squealed.

"And how!" I said. We drifted over to John and Robert. Robert nudged me in the shoulder, and I grinned. John and I spent the next hour holding hands, and touching each other. My feelings were too big.

I felt like I was floating as I said good night to my guests. I meandered to my room, my emotions simmering. I replayed the evening over and over in my head as I wrote in my new journal.

Dear Diary,

I can't believe John asked me to go steady with him!
I'm pinching myself. And Dorothy's face when John shot
her down. Priceless. I love her, but it was luscious to have
the guy she wanted for a change. Nancy's such a doll. What
would I do without her friendship? Life is perfect!!!

Pulling the covers around me, I clutched John's ring as I
fell asleep, keeping it my secret for a little while.

CHAPTER 2
Pearl Harbor

The next morning, my family walked home from church. The California sunshine soaked into my skin. Timmy raced around me, chanting, "Margaret's got a boyfriend."

"Mother, make him dry up." I checked to see who else was listening.

"Is he right?" my mother teased.

"The little snoop snuck into my party last night," I said. People stared. I wanted to disappear into the sidewalk. We lived near the church, and our neighbors attended services, including the Wilsons. The Satos and we were the only Japanese families in a twelve-block area, but many nationalities lived around us. There were several German and Italian families, a few Chinese, and one black family in our neighborhood. Mrs. Jenkins lived two houses from us, and her skin was the color of fudge. Her husband had died when their children were very little. I babysat for her every week.

"That is enough, Timmy," Mother said, smiling.

My sister, Barbara, and her husband, Howard, always spent Sundays at our house. When we arrived home, we scattered. Mother and Barbara filed into the kitchen. Robert and Timmy raced to the backyard with Trixie. Father relaxed in the front room, savoring "Sammy Kaye's Sunday Serenade," one of his favorite programs. Howard joined him. Because he worked long hours in his orchard, listening to the radio was a luxury Father didn't enjoy very often.

"I'll hang up your jacket, Father."

My father and his brother came to America together and fell in love with its freedom. They worked several jobs, saving enough money to purchase some land along the southern coast of California. Because they were Japanese immigrants, they weren't allowed to become citizens. Non-citizens couldn't own land. A Caucasian man—their former boss—purchased an acreage for my father and uncle, with the terms that the land be turned over to my brother and oldest cousin when they reached eighteen. Born in this country, they could own land. The Yamaguchi Brothers Orchard sprouted into existence, as a labor of love. Fruit grew there that amazed old-time farmers of the region.

As I shuffled toward the kitchen, I pecked my father's cheek. I loved preparing Sunday lunch with my mother and sister. It was cozy. Since Barbara had married and left the house, I missed seeing her every day. The three of us tied on aprons.

"Margaret, would you wipe the table, please?" Mother asked.

Exasperated, I looked at Barbara and rolled my eyes. I knew what to do! But I checked my words. In many ways, my life was opposite my mother's. Even though she left Japan years ago, some of her actions were very rooted in Japanese customs, such as waiting on the men and continual cleaning. *I* wanted to be a writer.

I received high marks and praise for my writing efforts in school. Mrs. Grady allowed me in journalism a year early. I helped write the grade-school plays and proofread the church newsletter for Reverend Bishop.

I didn't want to be just a wife and a mother. I didn't see the point of some of my mother's ways. Barbara was somewhere in between. Most Sundays, she was the buffer between Mother and me.

"John Wilson, you like?" Mother asked.

"Very much," I gushed.

"He is quite handsome. Polite. Helpful." Mother handed me the salad bowl.

I rinsed greens. "I can date now?"

"We will allow it." Mother sounded unsure. A small frown spilled onto her face.

"But what?" I prompted, afraid of what I'd hear.

Mother looked at me. "Boys can be dangerous creatures to young girls."

"It's different for me than it was for you."

Mother grinned. "When your father came to America, he was eighteen. Two years later, he looked at several pictures of young girls from Japan."

"And he selected you to be his bride." I adored their story. Father picked the right woman. They loved each other right away.

"We did not meet before the ceremony," Mother said.

"I wouldn't want that," I said. "What if you didn't like the person you married?"

"I am sure that happened." Mother coated chicken with flour and salt.

I stared at the woman who gave me life. Sometimes the reality of her childhood clashed with the reality of mine. I marveled at her willingness to give up the life she knew to move to another country.

"Was it difficult for you to watch us grow up so different than you did?" I asked. "You left behind so many things when you came here." Her life in Japan fascinated me, because I'd never been to the country. She left her family. She moved here to marry my father and never returned. Instead, she adapted to a new culture.

"My life is good. But I do not want you to marry so young as I did," Mother said.

"I'm going to college."

"I want you safe, Margaret. Happy."

"I am," I assured her. "John's heaven sent."

"His parents do not mind we are Japanese?"

"John and Robert have been friends since first grade."

"A friend and a girlfriend are not the same."

"That's not true." My anger flared.

Mother continued frying chicken.

With my heart slamming against my chest, I slipped the necklace out from under my blouse. I glanced briefly at Barbara, who stared with wide eyes. "John gave me this last night."

Mother turned. Her eyes focused on the ring, but her face gave no recognition of the jewelry. "Is this an intention of marriage?"

I giggled. "It means we'll date."

"I trust you will make the right decisions."

Relief swept over me. "I won't be foolish. John won't hurt me."

"You know this?" Mother teased.

"Robert would kill him if he did."

Mother laughed and squeezed me.

At 11:30, Father ran into the kitchen and turned on the radio.

We interrupt this program for an urgent news report. Japan has bombed Pearl Harbor. I repeat, Japan has bombed Pearl Harbor.

I dropped the salad bowl into the sink and stared at the radio. "Why would they do that? We aren't even in the war."

Father looked grim. "We are now."

The radio announcer continued:

Approximately thirty minutes ago, the Japanese air force attacked U.S. military and naval facilities on Oahu in the Hawaiian Islands. There was no warning for this attack. Lives were lost.

Mother put her hands to her mouth.

"What's going to happen?" I asked.

"We must wait and see," Father said. "We cannot avoid the war now."

"We're a neutral country! Why did Japan bomb us?"

"Perhaps to show strength by bombing the strongest country," Father said.

"Will they bomb the Coast?" Mother asked. "California?"

"We are safe. We are in America," Father said.

I re-rinsed the greens. "What happens to Robert if we enter the war?" I didn't want my brother, or John, to be drafted.

"He could not be drafted until he completes high school," Father said.

"We must have faith, Margaret," Mother said.

Barbara grabbed Howard's hand.

"I am ashamed to be Japanese," my father said quietly.

"I am also," Mother admitted. "Japan is the country of my birth, but I am now American. Even if they would not allow us to become *shimin*."

"You mean citizens?" I asked.

Father nodded. "We must not speak Japanese. We must show our allegiance now more than ever."

"This isn't your fault," I said.

My parents spoke only English to us, except for my mother. When she got excited or upset, she lapsed into Japanese. We kids never learned the language, except for a few phrases and our own names.

Mother stood straighter. "Father is right."

"We must call our family in Japan," Father said, putting his arms around Mother.

The radio blared.

> *Manila is being attacked by Japanese forces. I repeat, Japan is taking Manila.*

"I hate war." I sat down heavily. "Why can't the leaders of countries work out their problems? Why do they go to war?" I wrote the questions in my notebook.

"It is senseless," my father said.

"Will we really enter the war?" I asked.

"America has been attacked. There must be retaliation."

My heart sank.

Robert and Timmy ran inside, acting like a couple of knuckleheads.

"We've been bombed by Japan!" I cried.

The radio seemed to come to life.

Burma is under attack. Japan has taken hold of the Pacific. We don't have a casualty count at this time. Only that it is grim.

"They can't do that!" Robert shouted.

"They have," I whispered.

CHAPTER 3
Phone Calls

As my family hovered around the radio, the hall phone rang. I jumped. Father answered the call, patting my shoulder. I felt his fingers tremble slightly.

"Hello? Yes, Nancy, we are listening. Is it not a tragedy? Margaret is here."

Still clutching my notebook, I sat down on the hall steps. "Nancy?"

"Is this really happening?" Nancy asked.

"Father says we'll be in the war for sure now."

"My dad said so too. I can't stay on the phone long. Mother's going to call my grandparents in Japan."

"Most of our family is clustered around Hiroshima. What do you think will happen to them?" I asked.

"My parents are so worried they'll be bombed," Nancy said.

"I've never met my grandparents or aunts and uncles in Japan, but my parents write to them and try to phone when they can."

"I've seen my grandparents several times," Nancy said. "They're really old."

My heart ached for Nancy. "Take care of yourself, doll," I said.

"Gotta go, lamb pie. I'll see you in school tomorrow."

I hung up the phone and held Trixie. Nancy was always bubbly, carefree. I heard a commotion in the kitchen and rushed into the middle of an argument.

"I want to sign up," Robert said.

"No," Father said sternly. "You must finish high school."

"I'm not afraid, Father."

"You must finish schooling, then I will understand if you want to fight in this war."

Robert stomped off to use the phone.

"You won't let him leave school, will you?" I asked, clutching my chest, afraid of Robert's going off half-cocked.

"Robert will see that this is best." Father patted my shoulder again. "But I know his feelings. If I were a young man, I would consider joining the army."

I glanced at my older brother, sitting in the same position at the phone where I was moments before. Robert was stubborn and bossy, but he was also good-hearted. He looked out for me. I couldn't bear losing him in a war.

"Margaret," Robert called. "Someone wants to talk to you." He teased me with the phone, then relented.

"Hello?" I said quietly.

"Hi, beautiful," John said.

My heart melted. I forgot about the radio announcements and pictured John. "Hi yourself."

"Jeepers! Robert's mad."

"He wants Father to let him join the army."

"That's what he told me."

"Do you want to join?" I asked casually.

"We should finish high school. Another six months, and the war might be over."

I breathed a sigh of relief. "Robert values your judgment."

"I value his. But now I have another reason to spend time with him," John said.

"What's that?"

"You."

I twirled John's ring and smiled. "Want to come over?"

CHAPTER 4
War

The next morning, Robert, John, Nancy, and I walked to school. The only difference between that morning and countless others before was that John held my hand. I was his girlfriend!

At school, many of the girls noticed John and me together. My cousin Dorothy was one of those girls.

"Hi, Margaret," she called. "Hi, John," she cooed sweetly, pushing her way between John and me. "Walk me to class?"

"Hi there, playmate," John flirted. "My sweetheart would be sore." John reached in front of Dorothy, grabbed my hand, and pulled me close.

She stared as we strolled into the building. I couldn't help smiling. She was usually the girl with the cute boy. And she had been after John since school started. For once in my life, I had an edge over my popular cousin.

Our studies involved war-related activities and lessons. In political science, we studied the effects that World War I had on the global economy. We wrote essays about patriotism in English. The journalism class planned that week's paper around the war. As a sophomore, I was lucky to have a column.

"Mrs. Grady, I have a couple of ideas." I sat down near her desk. "During the radio report about Pearl Harbor, the thing that really griped me was how futile war is."

"How so?" Mrs. Grady listened.

"Can't the leaders of quarreling countries talk out their problems? If regular people started shooting others they fought with, they'd be put into jail!" I felt myself getting angry. "Why aren't countries held to the same levels of conduct?"

"Work up an editorial on that."

By the end of the morning, my mind was crammed with facts about previous wars. Fears about the current war kept brimming to the surface. As usual, the four of us sat together at lunch. Only this time, John and I sat next to each other. He played footsie with me under the table.

I surveyed the room. "Why are so many debs looking at us?"

Nancy grinned. "Because of you and John."

"Nancy's right," Robert said. "It's obvious you two are keeping company."

"Don't you want us to?" I asked Robert.

"You're my little sister." Robert put down his sandwich. "John's my best friend. You two are a smooth couple."

"Then what?"

"You're a sophomore. John and I are seniors. The other girls probably figured you were with us because of me. They resent you for taking John out of circulation."

John sputtered. "You make me sound like a contender in a horse race."

Robert laughed. "Some debs are jealous of Margaret. They're slack happy over John, and now he's not available."

I felt myself turning red and hot. John draped his arm around me. "I don't buy your brother's theory. I'm *not* the Casanova of Valle Verde High." John looked at Robert then back at me. "You're my baby, right?"

I nodded, wishing Robert and Nancy weren't around.

"Want to take a walk?" John asked.

My hand was a perfect fit for his larger one. I felt safe and happy. "It's a simply perfect day, isn't it?" I asked, gazing at the sky.

"And how. I'm finally able to be with you."

I knew John was looking at me and didn't know what to do. Was falling in love supposed to make me so nervous? "I always thought I was just Robert's sister to you."

"For a long time, you were. But that changed." We sat on the steps. "I've been dizzy for you for two years."

My eyes widened. "Two years?"

John wrapped me into his arms, pulling me gently into his shoulder. "You're the most beautiful girl I've ever seen *and* Robert's little sister. I had to play by the rules."

"But, you've dated so many girls! What about them?"

"Just biding my time."

"How do I know you're not doing that with me?" I asked.

John tilted my head back, leaned into me, and kissed me. His lips were firm yet gentle. I felt his hands along my cheeks as he pushed his mouth against mine. Then his tongue slipped between my lips. No one had ever kissed me so perfectly!

"I wouldn't have waited two years for any of the others, Margaret. They were nice to look at. Some were floozies. But they were mostly dumb Doras." John put his lips next to my ears. "I want a girl who's beautiful and intelligent. One with the goods. I want you."

I melted against him. A shrill ringing filled the courtyard. We walked hand-in-hand to the door. "I've got English." John pecked my cheek. "Bye, beautiful."

I stood in the middle of the hallway until Nancy grabbed my arm and tugged me into our room. "Margaret, we can't be late for math."

I palmed my cheek. The spot where John kissed me felt warm.

"I saw the smooch," Nancy said as we slid into our seats. "Details, lamb pie."

"Me too," Elizabeth Parks said.

All the debs chattered to me. Was this how it felt to be popular? Being John's girlfriend did this? I was overwhelmed by the attention and relieved when our lesson started. I tried to concentrate, but my fingers returned to John's necklace.

At two o'clock, we were herded into the gymnasium for an announcement. Our principal looked ill. "President Roosevelt signed a declaration of war against Japan. The United States has officially entered World War II." The roomed buzzed. "We're releasing you early. Go straight home."

I held on to John's hand as if my life depended on it.

"Are you okay, Margaret?" John asked.

"I can't breathe in here."

He ushered me to the nearest door. I gulped in the fresh air. "We're at war."

"Puts a different perspective on things," John said. "Sure you're okay?"

"It was just too much inside there."

A couple of debs walked by. "Hi, John," they waved.

"Blackout girls!" John teased.

"Babysitting?" they asked, eying me up and down.

"Something like that." John grinned as the girls strolled away.

I felt out of place. "Babysitting?" I asked.

"I didn't mean anything by it," John said.

"It makes me feel like a chunk of lead."

"I'm a louse." John kissed me softly.

"Can I ask you something?" I said.

"Sure." John sat down on the steps, pulling me with him.

"Do your parents approve of us dating?"

"Why wouldn't they?"

"It's just something my mom mentioned. She and my dad are Japanese . . ."

John cradled my face in his hands. "Margaret, my parents know your family. Same as your parents know mine. Nothing has changed."

"Except we're dating."

"Even if my parents didn't approve, nothing could keep me away from you."

I smiled and leaned my forehead into his. "I'm glad to hear you say that."

"Look at the lovebirds," chirped Nancy as she and Robert joined us on the steps. "Thought maybe you were off necking."

I blushed and gave Nancy a look. John laughed. As the four of us walked home, I realized Nancy liked Robert. The way she looked at him and tried to position herself near him made it obvious.

"Afternoon, Mr. Dennis," Robert said as we passed his yard.

"Don't walk so close to my house," Mr. Dennis grumped at us.

My mouth dropped open. "Mr. Dennis is always friendly." I pushed my hand further into John's. We dropped Nancy off.

"Hello, Mrs. Anderson," I said as we passed her driveway.

She didn't smile; she turned toward her house.

"How odd," I said. "She's usually so chatty."

"Strange mood," John said. "Must be the war announcement."

"You're probably right," I agreed. "And we're getting home early."

When we arrived at our house, Robert said, "Don't be mugging out here long, you two." He left John and me on the steps. We waved to Mrs. Jenkins, who was sweeping her front steps.

"Isn't it terrible about us joining the war?" Mrs. Jenkins said.

"It's awful," John said as I nodded.

"At least neighbors stick together." Mrs. Jenkins smiled. "See you kids later."

Mrs. Jenkins disappeared into her house. She cleaned houses during school hours, so she could be home when her kids were home. John played with my hair.

"I'm glad kids were staring," John said. "They noticed that we're together."

"It's super holding your hand." I thought I might pass out.

John French-kissed me. "Until tomorrow." He ran through Mrs. Jenkins' yard to his house.

My family was again around the radio. I glanced at Robert, who winked and made a kissing face. I went through the motions of helping with dinner, eating, and homework. My mind was torn between John and war. I pulled out my diary.

> *I'm so full of luscious feelings. Could John actually mean what he said? That he wouldn't have waited for another girl? But he really didn't WAIT, did he? I don't care. All that matters is he wants ME! Above Dorothy. Above the other debs in school. Maybe I am special enough. I always thought I was a nobody. Nancy always got the attention, and Dorothy always got the guy. Maybe being me is enough to have gotten John. Maybe I've got the goods.*

John phoned at eight o'clock. "Wanted to wish you swell dreams."

"They'll be wonderful tonight."

"Hope I didn't frighten you today, saying those things," John said.

"No, you didn't frighten me. You surprised me."

"In a good way?"

"Definitely." I hung up the phone and floated toward my room.

Robert stopped me in the hall. "I'm happy you're happy. About John, I mean."

"I'm over the moon!" I gave him a quick hug. "I'm not trying to come between you and John."

"You're not." Robert smiled. "You two are the bee's knees."

I was relieved Robert approved. "Do you like anyone?"

Robert shrugged. "Maybe." He turned toward his room, then stopped. "Do you think Nancy would go out with me?"

"I think she's got the hots for you."

I slipped into bed that night in turmoil, relishing my intense feelings for John. I suspected he felt the same about me. If he and Robert were drafted, the months ahead might be filled with goodbyes. I forced myself to think about good things. About John.

CHAPTER 5
Words

"Good morning, Father," I said as I sat down at the breakfast table.

"Good morning, Margaret. The news this day is not pleasant."

I stared at the *Valle Verde Gazette* in my father's hands. The headlines were full of President Roosevelt's address to Congress. Seeing it in print made the war more real.

Sunday, December 7, 1941, the United States of America was viciously attacked by Japan.

"We must be prepared for our lives to change," Father said.

I continued reading the report of President Roosevelt's address to Congress.

This attack took planning and strategy of several weeks. During that planning, the Japanese Government has assured the United States that Japan was striving for lasting peace between our countries.

I pushed my plate away as the words sunk into my head. This wasn't a game or practice. This was real. I swallowed hard and fought the fear rising in my throat.

Our country's freedom is at risk. If our citizens stand be-hind the United States armed forces, our nation cannot fail. Since Sunday, December 7, 1941, the United States has been at war with Japan.

I slid the paper back toward my father. He looked calm—not angry or scared like me. He accepted the war in the same way he had accepted leaving his country and family and adapting to a new culture.

"This frightens me," I confessed. "What if the war goes on for a long time?"

"We are not alone; we are part of an entire country."

"When you put it like that, it doesn't seem so scary."

"War is ugly, but we will get through this."

"Some fellows from my class enlisted yesterday," Robert said.

"We have discussed this," Father said. "You must wait until after graduation."

Robert and Father argued until we left for school. John walked me to my first class. Electricity crackled as we passed through the halls. I noticed whispers and stares more than the day before. With John, I was getting noticed. I was special.

"We're getting more looks today," John said.

"It must be your letterman's jacket."

"You think?"

"I always liked watching you when you wore it."

Like the day before, our lessons focused on war. In journalism, we worked hard to provide facts to the student body, but facts changed several times each day.

"Margaret," Mrs. Grady said. "I have two assignments for you. One is to write a summary of President's Roosevelt's speech tonight."

"And the other?" I asked.

"Historical background of the different Japanese generations."

"The Issei and Nisei?"

"And the Kibei. Explain the differences."

I spent journalism class researching. I wrote the background assignment first:

> *In the late 1800s, men and women from Japan came to America to further their educations and/or to escape poor economic conditions in some regions of Japan. This immigrant generation of Japanese are called the Issei. The Issei found jobs in agriculture, aqua culture, and timber industries, mostly along the West Coast. They prospered, despite obstacles such as long hours and poor working conditions. Many Issei men continued the custom of arranged marriages. Their "picture brides" were chosen after looking at photographs. This was how my parents met and married.*
>
> *Children of the Issei, the Nisei, are the first generation born in the United States and are American citizens by birth. Some Nisei, the Kibei, were educated in Japan. Most Nisei are all-American kids, with no personal ties to the country of Japan. Myself and my siblings were born here in Valle Verde. I have never been to Japan, and my parents haven't returned since their immigration to America.*
>
> *Children of the Nisei, the second generation born in the United States, are the Sansei. Most of the Sansei are babies or very young children.*

"My paper assignment for this week is incredibly huge," I said at lunch. "I have to write a summary of President Roosevelt's radio address tonight."

"Robert and I need to listen to it for political science," John said.

"Why don't you come over to our house?" I suggested.

"Nancy," Robert said, "Do you want to come too?"

Nancy gulped. "I'd love to."

Robert and John left for a class meeting, leaving Nancy and me alone.

"That's the first time your brother has ever asked me over," Nancy gushed.

"He's the drooly guy you like?"

Nancy turned red and nodded.

"He's the only boy you don't flirt with. I think you'd make a groovy couple."

"Robert's so dreamy. I didn't think he'd see me as anything but your friend."

I overheard some senior boys talking. "Dirty Japs. As soon as my orders come, I'm going to kill a bunch of them."

"My old man said to join up and mow down those slant eyes."

"Like I've heard, the only good Jap is a dead one."

What ugly words they used! Jap. It sounded dirty. Slant eyes. Is that how people saw me? I heard my heart pounding in my ears.

Nancy gripped my hand, her eyes huge. "Did you hear that?"

"Are they talking about us?" I whispered as the boys glared at us.

"How can they talk about shooting people like that!"

I felt numb. Not only were those boys using horrible words to describe my ancestors, they were talking about killing people, like life had no value. "I know that people die in war, but if Robert and John go, they'll be shooting people!" I whispered. I pushed my tray aside.

Nancy and I hustled out of the lunchroom, clutching each other's arms. Jap. Slant eyes. Dirty. They whirled around in my thoughts. I couldn't get those filthy words out of my head.

CHAPTER 6
The Privilege

John and Nancy arrived to listen to the radio address with my family.

"Hope it's okay we dropped over with John," Mrs. Wilson said to my mother.

"You are welcome in our home always." Mother embraced the Wilsons. Tingling, I embraced John. I led him to the floor beside the radio. Robert motioned for Nancy to sit beside him.

Uncle Toshio, Aunt Aiko, and my cousins, Steven and Dorothy, were already seated in the living room. My sister, Barbara, and her husband, Howard, also squeezed into the house. Trixie greeted each person with yips and a wiggle of the tail.

"John," Dorothy said sweetly, "There's room here." She scooted over to make a spot for John on the couch.

"I'm comfortable here, thanks," John winked at Dorothy, lacing his fingers through mine.

If the subject of the address weren't so frightening, it would have been a party. I sat quietly and held John's hand. I was excited about John's being with me and nervous about the task ahead. I was also getting angry with Dorothy.

John looked so relaxed, like part of our family. As I studied the different faces of the people seated around me, I wondered how war started. Why did people hate each other enough to kill?

"John, look what I can do," Timmy said over and over again. He pretended to play football and tackled John.

"That's pretty good," John said and lifted Timmy off him. "You'll be a tiger when you get into high school."

"I want to play football and basketball just like you."

"You'll be great." John tousled Timmy's hair.

Timmy plopped into John's lap, knocking his shoulder into me.

"Just sit down and clam up, Timmy," I snapped.

Mother clicked on the radio. I sat close to the speaker, pencil in hand, ready to record notes for my article. John settled himself beside me as the crackling began. President Roosevelt's voice captured our attention:

> *Citizens of the United States, recent criminal acts have been committed by the Japanese in the Pacific, following years of worldwide depravity. Japan has joined forces with Germany and Italy. Together, those countries challenge the United States of America. We accept that challenge.*

I couldn't get every word, but I had to retain the essence of the speech:

> *We must fight for our right to live freely. We must fight the immorality of the Axis nations, who view our world as conquerable.*

My stomach fluttered at those words. The entire world—my world—was at war. The war had seemed so distant to me. Now it was in my home.

> *We have entered this war. Americans, one and all, must stand together to fight the evil perpetrating Europe. We must help one another through this dark time in our nation's history.*

"I'm scared," Timmy cried. "What do I have to do?"

"Come here, buddy," Robert said. "You have to be brave. Can you do that?"

Timmy crawled onto Robert's lap as the president continued:

To those whose sons are serving in the armed forces: News will arrive in a timely manner.

Fire and desire radiated in Robert's eyes. He yearned to go to war. I couldn't picture him with a gun in his hand. Then I glanced at John. His eyes looked sad.

"Are you getting all this?" he whispered.

"I'm trying." I forced my thoughts back to the radio.

Ignore rumors you will undoubtedly hear. Enemy sources, citizens of Japan, are responsible for fabricating false reports.

My own grandmother was considered an enemy source! She lived in Japan, but she was an old woman. How could she be the enemy?

International communication must be refused during this war.

As I scribbled, I thought about my parents' families in Japan. The phone call two nights ago was the last one with their families until after the war. No phone calls, no letters, and no telegrams could be sent by private citizens now.

The newspapers and radio stations of our great country must uphold their responsibility. You must not report unsubstantiated accounts as truth. Every American citizen must also support this obligation.

For a moment, I felt as if President Roosevelt spoke to me. Although my work on a high school paper wasn't exactly Pulitzer Prize-winning work, it was important. Most of the kids at school didn't read the daily paper at home, but gobbled up our school news. I had to get this right.

I jotted down key words in my notebook as the president spoke: long war, hard war, basis of plans, how we measure what we'll need, production increasing for our own army and navy as well as armies and navies fighting with us.

My wrist ached, but I wrote as fast as I could. The president warned of hard work ahead, for the duration of the war. He started to say that there would be sacrifice, but then said that wasn't the correct word. It wasn't a sacrifice to do your best for your country, especially when at war. He said that it was a privilege to do without things that we are used to, if it means success in the war.

As I wrote, everyone in the room disappeared from my thoughts. I concentrated on the president's words and their meaning:

> *The United States will obtain victory. We have realized a vicious truth with the bombing of Pearl Harbor. As long as terrorism exists in our world, no nation is safe, no matter how remote the threat seems.*

I gripped the pencil tighter. We wouldn't be in this war if not for Japan. The president said that Americans are builders and not destroyers. I thought of Japan as a destroyer. I paraphrased the president's words about building a world that would be safe for children of this nation. That meant getting rid of the danger from Japan, and Hitler and Mussolini.

> *We will win this war. We will regain peace for our country. Most nations of the world support our efforts and pray for our victory; it is their victory as well.*

John squeezed my shoulder. Only then did I realize how tense I felt.

"A stirring speech," Father said.

"I hate the Japanese," Robert said.

"You hate the people of Japan?" I asked.

"The goons that bombed us and dragged us into war."

What was the difference between hating war and hating the people at war? I jotted the question in my notebook, then closed the cover.

All the adults started yakking at once. Mother clicked off the radio. I dragged John into the kitchen and pulled plates out of the cupboard. "President Roosevelt said it's going to be a long war." I avoided John's eyes.

"Robert and I will probably fight in it."

"I'm afraid of that." My throat burned. "I'm more afraid of losing you."

John embraced me. "Let's not worry about it until graduation."

Everyone crowded into the kitchen for cocoa and cookies. Would the months ahead feel like a sacrifice or a privilege?

CHAPTER 7
December Blessings

On December 12, the paper reported that the FBI had detained 1,370 Japanese Americans classified as "dangerous enemy aliens."

"What does that mean?" I asked. "Dangerous enemy aliens."

Father shook his head. "Perhaps people closely tied to Japan."

My stomach flip-flopped. Could there be that many dangerous enemies here?

The next day, after my father's weekly trip to the bank, he found out all our money was frozen. "All Japanese assets are off limits."

"You could draw no money?" Mother asked.

"Bank accounts are frozen. We cannot have our money."

"Horsefeathers!" I cried. "It's our money."

"Our safe deposit box was confiscated." Father sat down heavily, but his face remained calm and proud.

"What will we do?" I asked. Because of Father's business, we didn't have a monthly income. Our money came in large amounts in the spring and summer. My parents deposited the sums, then drew out spending money each week.

"This is America," Father said. "This is just a mistake."

"It's like *we're* the enemy!" I stormed to my room and wrote in my notebook:

> *As a minority in the Valle Verde High School, I must draw to the student body's attention the fact that I am as much an American as anybody else. I was born in this country; I know no other culture. I have no divided allegiance.*
>
> *My parents emigrated from Japan many years ago, to give their children a better life. If they had been allowed to become citizens of the United States, they would have. The laws of this country, my country, prevent my parents the honor of citizenship.*
>
> *I am proud to be an American. My older brother plans to join the ranks of the enlisted and fight for the freedom of this country. I love this country and what it stands for— Lessons from my father. My family has done nothing to arouse suspicions, and yet we are being treated as if we are the enemy. When you leave school today, ask yourself why. We are moral, honest members of this community. We have shown and will continue to show our unwavering patriotism to the United States.*

As I finished what I hoped would be the next editorial for the school paper, I dialed Mrs. Grady's home number. Then I called Nancy.

"Margaret, you'll never guess what happened," Nancy said breathlessly.

"Did your bank accounts get frozen too?"

"What?"

"Our accounts and our safe deposit box are off limits to us."

Silence filled the phone line.

"Sorry, doll, I thought you knew." Sometimes I forgot that Nancy didn't enjoy knowing all the details of life like I did. She preferred to enjoy life and let someone else take care of the details, especially if they involved politics.

"Do you think they'll be frozen a long time?" Nancy asked.

"Father says it's just a mistake." I bit my lip. "What were you going to tell me?"

"Oh, Margaret," Nancy gushed. "Robert asked me to go steady."

"Hot dog, Nancy! Let's all go out during Christmas break."

"I am so stuck on him, Margaret. He's so romantic!"

"Robert?!" I squealed. "Applesauce!"

"I'm on the level, lamb pie. And, he's an educated fox."

"He hasn't dated that much," I giggled.

"He's dated enough," Nancy said.

"I think I've heard enough," I laughed. "I'll never be able to look at my brother again with a straight face."

"Okay," Nancy said. "Now, spill the beans on John."

"Well, he's a super kisser," I whispered.

"And?"

"And we haven't done anything else."

"From what I've heard, he's been on active duty for a few years." Nancy lowered her voice. "Mary Smith used to date him, and she said he's definitely educated. Can you believe it?"

"She's all wet," I said. But I wondered about the rumors.

I hung up the phone. The next few days were filled with anxiety and tension.

Mrs. Grady ran my editorial, in a special edition of the *VV Sentinel*. She asked my permission to submit it to the *Gazette* as a letter to the editor. I stared at my name in print for the first time. I absolutely had to be a writer.

On December 24, I read the morning paper with increased interest.

Despite uncertainties due to Japanese attacks against the United States, the Nisei, American-born children of Japanese immigrants, insist that their future is in America.

Some Nisei have encountered discrimination in their own homeland. They were born here and are U.S. citizens by that birthright, but are viewed, especially on the West Coast, as intruders. Many have no ties to Japan, except for their parents. Many have never traveled to the country and know only American values and culture.

The vast majority of those who moved from Japan truly love this country and are of no threat to national security, but restrictions may be needed to insure everyone's safety. If Americans look at this fairly, no innocent people will be hurt.

Part of the story defended my editorial, but the last paragraph bothered me. What restrictions could be placed on citizens who have committed no crimes?

We were out of school early on Christmas Eve. I spent part of that evening with John's family. His parents gave me a beautiful sweater. Being with them felt like being in a second home.

John gave me earrings to match my birthday pin. I gave him *Between Two Worlds* by Upton Sinclair. Inside, I drew a forget-me-not and wrote:

> For John,
> May we always be this happy.
> Love, Margaret.

It was a simple Christmas. The government restored limited access to Japanese bank accounts, so we made presents. I wrote my mother a poem:

> Like an orchid rare
> plucked from its native ground
> You offer life joy.
>
> Like a wildflower
> roaming without boundaries
> I live in freedom.

Two distinct floras
thrive in an anchored garden.
From you my life blooms.

Mother cried, "It is beautiful, Daughter."

I made a ceramic cup for Father in the school art room, framed Robert's baseball award, and gave Timmy my toy rabbit he had always admired. My sister surprised us all.

"I'm pregnant," Barbara announced.

She and I went window-shopping one afternoon and chattered like we used to when she still lived at home. We strolled arm in arm downtown and giggled and laughed at silly things. Aside from Nancy, Barbara was my confidante.

"I'm so excited, Margaret," Barbara said. "I'm going to be a mother!"

"Are you scared?" I asked.

"A little. But mostly I'm happy."

She positively glowed. I couldn't wait to be an aunt.

"How are things between you and John?" Barbara asked.

"I love him, Bar," I gushed. "I haven't told anybody, not even Nancy."

"He absolutely adores you, too."

"How do you know that?"

"It's all over his face," Barbara said. "Have you two . . . you know?"

"No! Why would you say that?"

"Just be careful, Mar." Barbara looked into my eyes. "He might be more . . . experienced."

"That's jive, Barbara. John wouldn't do that to me."

"Don't get in a lather," Barbara said. "I'm not pointing fingers. I'm just worried."

"Why?"

"I love you. You're sweet and pretty and trusting. Sometimes, when you're all those things, you get hurt."

"What happened to you isn't going to happen to me."

When Barbara was seventeen, she fell in love with a college boy. They dated for several months, and when she wouldn't
sleep with him, he started wolfing on the side. She saw him
out one night with a floozie. They were in the back seat of his
car. Devastated, she didn't date anyone for over a year, until
she and Howard started going steady.

In all, Christmas was a happy time. I was falling in love. I
felt it could be my only love. Such a feeling was so overpower-
ing, at times it frightened me.

Christmas vacation was scheduled to last until January 5,
so John, Robert, Nancy, and I planned several outings together.
We skated on the pond, caroled through the neighborhood,
and made decorations in our basement.

"Let's go for a drive," John said one afternoon. He pulled
me outside, then slid to the passenger side of the car.

"What are you doing?" I asked.

"It's time you started driving. Hop in."

"Robert was going to teach me next summer."

"It isn't hard, Margaret." John showed me how to start the
car, what the pedals were for, and made me drive around the
block about twenty times.

"I'll treat you to a soda if you get us downtown."

I drove, achingly slowly, to the diner on Elm. I parked,
then blew my breath out.

"Now you can drive," John said.

"But I don't have my license."

"A technicality."

After our soda, I drove to the orchard. "Father's gone
home," I said, disappointed.

"Good," John said. "We're alone."

I was excited and scared all at once when John seized
me in his arms. I wanted to keep feeling so tingly, but I didn't
want to be a charity girl. I broke the embrace. "We'd better get
back."

"Not yet," he said gently. His hands crept under my coat. I didn't know what to do. When he tugged on my blouse, I sat up.

"John, I can't. Not yet."

"You're not teasing, are you?"

"I'm just not ready." I felt tears coming.

"It's okay." John pulled me back into his arms and kissed my forehead. "I didn't mean to scare you."

Confused, I let him hold me and felt like a prude. "I'm sorry, John."

He kissed my eyebrow. "Don't be sorry. I don't want to push you into anything. I just have squirrel fever, being next to you."

"Have you . . . before?" I asked.

John nodded. "Sure. You haven't?"

I shook my head, feeling very warm.

"When it's the right time, we will."

I kissed him and ran my hands through his hair.

"I won't be able to stop if we don't go," John mumbled.

I took a deep breath then started the car. We drove home, smoldering lust pushing on me from every direction. I parked the car, baffled by my conflicting emotions. I wanted John to kiss me and touch me, but I didn't want to lose control.

"You send me, Mar," John said, kissing me lightly. "Send me straight to the stars." He walked me to my door. Why did his words fluster me?

Robert and John had a bit of scratch saved up, so they treated Nancy and me to *Meet John Doe* at the drive-in in Mr. Wilson's old car.

"This car is such a struggle buggy," Nancy chuckled from the back seat.

I blushed, knowing she and Robert were boodling behind us. I hugged my arms around my waist and hinged a glance at John. Did he expect the same thing?

He wrapped his arm around me and kissed my hair. "Don't be nervous," he whispered. "I don't want a petting party."

"Don't they make you uncomfortable?" I asked into his ear.

"I'm not on the make, Margaret. I'll wait for you to be ready."

I initiated a French kiss. I scooted closer to him and put my head on his shoulder. We watched the movie, ignoring the giggles and noises from the backseat.

The next morning, John invited me to his house.

"These cookies are for your mom," I said, stepping into the kitchen.

"She's shopping." John smirked. "We've got some homework to do." John leaned over, pinning me in my chair. He kissed me deeply, forcing me to gasp for air.

"John, wait," I said. My body froze.

"Come on, Mar," John said softly. "I just want to touch you."

"I'm not a bimbo," I argued, pushing his hands away.

"I know you're not a bimbo. This won't mean you are one."

"John, please, I'm scared."

John pulled his hands away and plopped into a chair. "Don't you trust me?"

"I've got to get to Mrs. Jenkins," I stammered and ran out the door. I babysat for her every afternoon. I had saved most of my babysitting money from the summer and by Christmas had enough to buy myself a typewriter—my first "big" purchase.

I wrote several drafts for the paper about subjects that were important to me: the growing prejudice in our community, anti-Japanese hysteria sweeping the country, and the ignorance of our leaders—lumping everyone who looked Japanese into the same category as the enemy. I typed them on my new machine. I also wrote in my diary for hours.

Dear Diary,

What do I do about John? He wants to have sex. I can't believe I'm even thinking about it. But I am. I want him to be my lover. But I don't want to be stupid. We haven't been dating a month yet. He said he understands, but he's also pushing a bit. I like kissing and touching him. Would it be so horrible to go all the way? I always thought it should be with the man I loved. I do love him. What if he goes to war? I can't talk to Nancy. She's all hotsie totsie for the boodling. She probably thinks we already have. I need to wait and still hang on to John. Mary Smith is called a floozie around school. I couldn't bear to have that label.

Christmas vacation was full of romance and promise. I loved spending it with John.

As I fell asleep on December 27, I tried to think like my father. I counted my blessings. We were free people. We were Americans. My family was loving and strong. As long as we remained together, I could cope with anything.

CHAPTER 8
Enemy Aliens

The headlines December 28 flashed:

ENEMY ALIENS TO SURRENDER CAMERAS AND SHORT WAVE RADIOS.
Every enemy alien—every Japanese, German, or Italian citizen—in the county must turn over their cameras and short wave radios to the police or sheriff's office to prevent radio messages being sent and received on the West Coast.

"Father, according to this article, any citizen of Japan, Germany, or Italy is an enemy alien." I pointed at the *Gazette.* "It implies you're an enemy!"

"I am not."

"You're going to turn over your camera?"

"I do not have a choice, Margaret."

"This is so stupid."

"It will be okay." Father patted my hand.

The following morning, the insult deepened. Headlines read:

CONTRABAND SEIZED FROM ENEMY ALIENS

The article stated all contraband be surrendered. Property seen as threats included: binoculars, hunting knives, and dynamite used by farmers to clear their land. California, Idaho, Montana, Nevada, Oregon, Utah, and Washington were all affected.

"My parents are considered enemy aliens," I confided to John. My stomach lurched. "They're viewed as the enemy by the government's definition."

"But they're not, Margaret," John said, squeezing my hand. "If the government would have allowed your folks to become citizens, they'd be citizens."

"What gripes me is, I'm called a *non-alien*." I clenched my teeth. "What piffle! I'm an American citizen!"

"It's bushwa." John pushed my hair back. "You're wearing the earrings?"

"Every day," I said, some of my anger leaving. "And your ring."

"It's your ring now."

Uncle Toshio's family came over for dinner on the last day of 1941. Dorothy sidled up to John. "Hi there, devil." She pecked his cheek, leaving a red lipstick print. "I didn't wish you a Happy New Year yet."

She slipped away to the bathroom, and I trailed her. I slammed the door behind me. "Leave him alone!" I screamed.

"John's not your property, Mar," Dorothy said as she checked her lipstick. "Lighten up, dearie."

"He's *my* boyfriend!"

"I'll believe that when *he* says it." Dorothy skedaddled out the door.

On January 5, 1942, the list of confiscated items grew once again. Now it included firearms, weapons of any kind, ammunition, bombs, explosives and materials to make explosives, codes, any document or book that might have invisible writing, any photo, sketch, or drawing of anything military.

My father didn't hunt, but he had a gun given to him by a childhood friend. He dug the gun out from a box in the basement. "The government will quickly return our possessions, once they realize we are not against this country."

"Why don't you dummy up? They wouldn't even know!" I was furious he had to hand over his gun.

"That would be deceitful. I have nothing to hide."

"You look like a chump," I muttered.

While Father cleaned the gun, Robert and John ran downstairs. Robert shouted, "Look what the eels did!"

I took the piece of paper from him. The War Department had classified draft-age Japanese American men as enemy aliens (class 4C), rather than eligible draftees.

"A few of the Japanese American college students tried to register for selective service and were refused." Robert looked like he would explode. "Japanese American soldiers were discharged or assigned to menial labor because of this."

"I'm sorry," I said. That slip of paper marked him as the enemy. He couldn't enlist. One part of me was angry for his dismissal simply because of his name. But another part of me was relieved. I didn't want him to fight and die in a war. I glanced at my father. He silently polished his gun.

"They won't even give us a chance to prove our patriotism." Robert slammed his fist into the wall. "It's a double cross!"

"It doesn't make any sense." I inched closer to John.

"Robert wants to join and fight in the war, and they won't take him," John said. "I don't want to go to war, and I'll end up putting on the suit."

His words sent a shiver up my spine. I grabbed his hand.

"We're willing to risk our lives for everyone's freedom," Robert said. "Is the government afraid we'll try to sabotage that?"

"So many of the Japanese immigrants came to America to escape their lives in Japan," John said.

"Like our parents," I said.

"They wouldn't work and live in this country for twenty years then suddenly turn to spying for a country they left," John said.

"The government must believe they would," Robert said. "Or teach their children to. For crying out loud, I've never been to Japan. Why would I be loyal to that country?"

"I can't believe the army would turn away those willing to fight," I said.

"I want to prove I'm an American," Robert said slowly. "The finks knocked off my chance." Robert stormed out of the house.

CHAPTER 9
JACL

That evening, Robert came home with his arms full of paperwork from the JACL. In 1930, the Nisei formed the Japanese American Citizens League to be accepted as Americans.

"This group is influential in California, Oregon, and Washington," Robert said, "where the majority of Japanese and Japanese Americans live."

"What does this group do?" Father asked.

"Fights Japanese discrimination; shows America that Nisei are loyal."

"How?" I asked.

"Members recite a pledge and show by example that Japanese are loyal."

"Did you join?" Father asked.

Robert nodded. "The army doesn't want me, maybe I can prove my loyalty this way."

"What does the pledge say?" I asked.

Robert handed me a piece of paper:

I am proud that I am an American citizen of Japanese ancestry, for my very background makes me appreciate more fully the wonderful advantages of this nation. I believe in her institutions, ideals, and her future. I am firm in my belief that American sportsmanship and attitude of fair play will judge citizenship and patriotism on the basis of action and achievement and not on the basis of physical characteristics.

"Has the JACL done any good?" I asked.

"Some," Robert said. "But they need as many new members as possible now."

"Because of the bombing?"

Robert nodded again. "Come with Nancy and me."

"Nancy joined?"

"There's a demonstration tomorrow."

Nancy had joined? This was the first political interest she had ever shown. And the first time she did something without telling me.

"I want to come," Timmy said.

"You're too young," Robert replied.

"Ah nuts!" Timmy stalked to his room.

The phone rang, and I ran to answer.

"Hi there, playmate," John said. "Want to join me tomorrow for a game of basketball?"

"I can't," I said. "There's a JACL rally."

"Then I'll join you."

"It's for Japanese Americans."

"Oh," John said. "See you when I see you, then."

Did I hurt John's feelings? I went to bed wondering if I had flubbed up. Would John break up with me?

The next day, alongside my brother and best friend, I marched down the main street of Valle Verde, waving an American flag and reciting the pledge I had memorized the night before. Rather than feeling stupid, I felt exhilarated. I was doing something, not just standing back letting things happen to me. Some of the white storeowners threw things at us and called us names, but there were hundreds of us marching! With that much support in one group, the insults couldn't bother me.

"Let's get John," Robert said, as we piled into his beat-up tin Lizzie.

I sat alone in the backseat. Was John mad at me?

Robert parked the car and ran to John's front door. John jumped into the backseat with me. He draped his arms over me.

"Hi." He nuzzled my neck.

"You're not mad?" I whispered.

"About what?"

"You couldn't come with us?"

"At first. But I didn't belong in the rally." He kissed me. "Don't worry so much. A little thing like that isn't going to get rid of me."

"Okay you two snuggle pups, this is a respectable rig. No boodling back there."

"Robert!" I cried.

He and John laughed and slapped hands. I shook my head at them. "I'm starved. Can we go to Manny's?"

"As you wish, my sister queen." Robert drove to our favorite hangout. We had burgers and malts, then apple pies. Then we drove to Strawberry Hill. There was only one other car there, and its windows were all fogged up.

"They've been busy," Nancy quipped. She scooted over to Robert and soon they were making out.

John looked into my eyes, raised his eyebrows, and leaned down to kiss me. I let him ease me back onto the seat and kiss my face all over. He unbuttoned my coat and slid it to the floor. He was so gentle and patient. He kissed my chin, slipping his own coat off.

He grazed my skin with his lips, down my jaw bones, my throat, then the top of my chest. My breath caught, but I didn't stop him. He whispered, "Only what you want."

I opened my eyes. The look on his face was one of desire, and something deeper. I saw him breathing hard. He smoothed my hair away from my forehead. I touched his hand

and felt it tremble. I couldn't help crying. He wiped the tears away. "What's wrong?"

"Nothing." I kissed his fingers and closed my eyes. Then he ran his fingers softly along my face, down my collar bone, to my blouse. He touched my shoulder and caressed the top of my breast. My heart sounded like galloping feet.

John moved his body, shielding me from the front seat. He unbuttoned my blouse and tugged it out of my skirt. His hand touched my bare skin, and a moan escaped my lips. "My oomph girl." John kissed my breasts.

He slid his fingers over the chain and his ring, his skin warm against mine.

I lifted John's sweater up. He jerked it and his T-shirt off. I rubbed his chest, his stomach, wanting to paw him all over. He closed his eyes, holding my hands against his heart. "Mar," he murmured. Then he stretched himself out on top of me.

We kissed again, this time harder. All of a sudden, I couldn't breathe. I panicked.

"I won't hurt you, Margaret," John pledged.

"I've got to slow down," I whispered. "This is happening too quickly."

John took a deep breath and kissed my stomach, sending shivers up my spine. "You're not teasing, are you?"

I shook my head. "I just need time. I haven't . . ."

John placed my hand against his fella. "It's taking a lot of control to stop."

I stroked him, shocking myself. John unhooked my bra. "Let me touch you?" We petted each other until Robert and Nancy started talking. John threw our coats over us, abruptly ending our make-out session.

"Ready?" Robert asked, pulling away from the parking spot.

As Robert drove, John and I dressed and giggled. Sharing such an intimate moment, I felt closer to him than anyone. We kissed, leaning back on the seat. Robert walked Nancy home, leaving us alone.

"Are you disappointed?" I asked.

"I want to make love to you, Margaret." John held my face in his hands. "But I want you to want the same thing."

Dear Diary,

We can make a difference! We really can. If we stick together and show our patriotism, things will be okay. The only thing I'm a bit concerned about is: John wasn't able to be a part of the JACL. Does that matter? WILL it matter? Isn't the fact we care about each other enough?

It seemed enough tonight. When he kisses me, I lose myself. I don't want to be a good girl. I want to tear his clothes off. I want to touch him and make him feel how he makes me feel. I can't believe I touched him! He touched me! Is this love?

CHAPTER 10
Restrictions

School resumed after the holidays. Hostility oozed from the other students. Debs that had been my friends since first grade were giving me the brush-off.

"You know," one of the more popular debs said loudly, "John Wilson is a Big Time Operator."

"A wolf! Called me just last night."

"Just using his little Jap quiff."

I dropped my eyes between classes, not acknowledging any of the jabs, although I was dying inside. Nancy and I hung close to each other.

"Come clean," I said to John at lunch. "Is what the girls are saying true?"

"What are they saying?" John said.

"You're still calling them. You're just using me for monking."

"I can't believe you're even asking me." John shook his head. "Don't you know me better than that?"

"No, I don't," I said. "I've known you most of my life as Robert's cute friend who has a new girlfriend every couple of months. I don't want to be the next one you use."

John sighed. "I'm not using you, Margaret. But you're right. I have to prove myself to you. And I will." He kissed my temple. "They're trying to break us up. Just ignore them."

49

"I can't ignore Dot," I cried. "My own cousin is trying to weasel her way to you."

"Dot's just dingy." John rubbed my shoulders. "Besides," John continued, "if I did anything improper, Robert would beat me to a pulp. Ask him, if you're worried."

John was probably right; I went to my first afternoon class.

My math teacher wouldn't call on Nancy or me. He just nodded his head at me during roll call, as if I were unworthy of his attention. I wiped a tear from the corner of my eye as Elizabeth slid a note onto my desk.

M—

I feel sick about what's happening. Can I do anything?

E.

She wanted to remain friends! On the back of her note, I wrote:

E—

Don't get in trouble. Give me a jingle tonight?

M.

At least Mrs. Grady was still the same. She listened to my ideas, and despite pressure from the principal to boot me off the paper, she stood by me. "I can't print all your articles, Margaret. You know why."

I nodded.

"I'll use some of them, to counter what these kids are hearing at home."

As January gained momentum, so did the biased feelings in the student body. I started hating school, unless I was in the journalism room. I didn't have to prove myself with the paper staff.

The editor of the *VV Sentinel* said, "Margaret, you're one of us."

Leaving school one day, John leaned down and kissed me.

A senior boy called out, "Hey, Jap lover!"

"Dry up!" John wrapped his arm around me protectively as we zipped away.

"Why do you date me?" I asked.

John turned to face me. "I've fallen in love with you, Margaret."

My mouth gaped. I couldn't speak. I wanted to shout to the world that John loved me, but all I could do was grab him and kiss him.

I suffered through my classes each day, ignoring kids who called me a gook or a Nip or a skibby. The repeated slurs eroded my resolve. I looked forward to lunch period. John and I ate outside, away from everyone. The days dragged by, and a burning in my stomach grew bigger every day. I dreaded the morning, starting each day, and began thinking up reasons to skip school.

One Saturday, John dragged me outside, to show me how to play basketball.

"I'm a klutz," I said.

"I've seen you dance," John said. "You're no klutz."

"When it comes to sports I am."

John showed me how to dribble, how to shoot a free throw, and a lay up.

After a couple of hours, I was drenched in sweat. "That was fun!"

John folded me in his arms. "Want to have some more fun?"

I kissed him, then pushed him away. "My mother is right inside the house."

"We can go somewhere else."

I leaned into him, shaking my head.

John threw the ball down. "Ish kabibble."

"This was a lovely afternoon; don't louse it up by getting in a lather," I pleaded.

"I want to be with you, Margaret, touch you, hold you, be alone with you."

I peered into his eyes. "And I keep telling you, I need time."
I picked up the basketball and handed it to him. "It's your shot."

John ran his hands through his hair, blew his breath out,
then grabbed the ball.

On January 28, the California State Personnel Board voted
to bar all descendants of natives with whom the United States
was at war from all civil service positions. Barbara worked in
the courthouse.

That evening, she and I took a walk. "I don't know what to
do," she said. "I was planning on quitting when I had the baby,
but I've never been fired from anything."

"It isn't because of you," I said. "It's our Japanese heritage. I know Mrs. Jenkins always needs help looking after her
kids. Talk to her."

The very next day, Attorney General Francis Biddle began establishing prohibited zones to secure the coast. The
zones were forbidden to all enemy aliens. All German, Italian,
and Japanese aliens were ordered to leave San Francisco
waterfront areas.

"Father, how can they do this? Where will these people
go?"

"I do not know. The government will soon see the error
and correct it."

As I read further in the *Gazette*, I saw that all Japanese,
German and Italian aliens aged fourteen years or older were
ordered to apply for certificates of identification.

"You and Mother will have to go next week and register," I
said to my father.

"Yes, I know."

"You are technically enemy aliens. You have to go to the
post office."

The January 30 *Gazette* mentioned again that aliens may
be moved from "vital areas" along the West Coast. The government was worried about the safety of the country. It was es-
timated that removal would affect at least one or two persons in

every local Japanese family, because the parents were almost entirely of Japanese birth, and therefore considered enemy aliens.

Earl Warren, attorney general of California, said, "Unless something is done, it may bring a repetition of Pearl Harbor." He called Japanese Californians the "Achilles heel of the entire civilian defense effort."

"This is ridiculous," I said. "You two are called enemy aliens while I'm considered a non-alien."

"The government is worried about Japan attacking the Coast," Father said.

"What does that have to do with us?"

"They are concerned about the good of the whole. If they must question us to make sure we are not spies for the Japanese, that is fine," Father said.

"But how would they test you?" I asked. I pushed myself up and grabbed my notebook. I had an idea for an article for the *Sentinel*:

Many native Californians are prejudiced against immigrants, like my parents. Some along the Coast feel the Japanese took jobs away from their families. But men like my father took land nobody else wanted and turned it into productive, fertile farmland in order to support his family. In 1940, farms in Washington, Oregon, and California averaged $37.94 per acre; Japanese farms averaged $279.96 an acre. Now that my father is successful, some want to blame him. For what? Being born in another country, coming to America, and living the American dream?

My father's not interested in taking away from anyone. Most Issei farmers in America, like my father, are truck farmers. They do not ship their crops to eastern markets like white farmers. Issei farmers are not in competition with white farmers. My father worked long hours and cultivated the soil to make his farmland some of the richest in California.

He wants to raise his family in peace. He taught me and my siblings how lucky we are to live in freedom in this country. Now, because he is from Japan, we might have to leave our home.

According to the 1940 alien registration, aliens in eight western states—California, Oregon, Washington, Montana, Idaho, Utah, Nevada, and Arizona—made up one-tenth of the Japanese, German and Italian aliens in the United States. The greatest number of aliens live in California, followed by Washington.

Many of you students have known me for ten years. Have you ever known me to be any different from you? Logic is giving way to hysteria, and families such as mine are caught in the middle.

Chapter 11

Rules and Exceptions

"Do you want me to go with you to register?" I asked my parents.

"No, Margaret," Father said. "We read and write English accurately."

"We do not rely on our children to communicate," Mother said proudly. My parents dressed in their church clothes, as they always did when they went out. They looked nifty. If I didn't know the reason for their outing, I would suspect they were going shopping then out to lunch.

My stomach was tied in knots, thinking about school. I wanted some excuse to stay home and avoid the ugliness. Robert was ready to put his life on the line to fight. I was too scared to go to school.

"Come on, lamb pie, we have to go to school. Don't you want to see your friends?" Nancy asked.

"What friends?" I demanded.

"Me."

"Why can't I be more like you?" I asked. I plodded to school with Nancy. I forced myself to tough it out, then practically sprinted out the doors at three o'clock. I had stopped attending John's basketball practice, so I staggered home with Robert and Nancy. Each day, I felt lonelier.

On February 3, the *Valle Verde Gazette* stated:

There will be no exceptions for those enemy aliens living in restricted areas. Some had hoped to remain with their children, who are citizens. After February 24, they will have to leave the areas. They cannot return to do their shopping. Most of the fields are in the restricted area, and aliens cannot go within the designated limits. Whether aliens will be required to pay taxes on the property they are not allowed to use has not been decided. Within these areas, aliens may not reside, work, or visit. The penalty is internment.

I felt physically ill at the thought of my parents being interned and jailed.

"So far, it does not affect us," Father said.

"Let us pray for those it does," Mother said.

The next morning, I read the army established twelve "restricted areas" in which enemy aliens had a 9 p.m. to 6 a.m. curfew. They could travel to and from work, and not more than five miles from their homes.

"Does this affect you?" I asked. "It's ten miles to the orchard."

"We have until February 24. The situation must change before then."

I stared at my father. "How can you be so certain?"

"Why should my faith falter?" he answered calmly. "This country provides life for my family. I am thankful."

"The government doesn't trust anybody from Japan."

"I have done nothing wrong."

I shook my head. I was confused. I felt anger at my father for being so complacent. Then I felt guilt for doubting him and for not being stronger, like both of my parents. Was I a coward?

Timmy sat down at the table, holding my diary.

"Give me that!" I screamed. I lunged at Timmy.

"Make me." Timmy held my diary just out of my reach.

"Father, make him give that back. That's my personal thing."

"Boy, is it!" Timmy grinned. "Want to hear about one of her dates with John?"

I erupted. "You little weasel. Hand it over!" I leaped out of my seat, bumped into him, and my diary flew out of his hand. I pounced on it. "If you ever go in my room again, ever touch this, I will make you very sorry you did."

"I'm quaking."

"Timmy, it is not polite to take Margaret's belongings," Mother said.

School that day was loathsome. By the final bell, I was wrung. I stepped outside, and it was raining pitchforks.

"Want to practice driving?" John asked.

"Sounds keen."

I slipped behind the steering wheel of John's car. He sat close to me, his arm around my shoulders. He smelled divine, like fresh country air.

"Take Main," John directed.

I eased the car into traffic and drove us through downtown past Maple, where the road turned to dirt. "Where are we going?"

"Just a couple more miles."

We parked in front of an old farmhouse.

"My mom grew up in that house," John said. "When my grandma died a few years ago, my folks thought about fixing it up, moving out here."

"Does your mom still own it?"

"They rent the land, but no one's lived in the house since Gran."

John led me to the front door. The porch creaked with our footsteps. I saw rotting wood, peeling paint, and disrepair. John saw something different. I squeezed his hand. When we went inside, spider webs snapped, and a blast of musty odors hit my nose. We poked around the rooms, then John led me upstairs.

"This is what I wanted to show you," John said, leading me into one of the bedrooms. On the floor a blanket was spread, a picnic basket waiting for us.

"When did you do this?" I asked.

"Skipped a couple of classes this afternoon."

I stood on tiptoes, kissed him, and curled myself into him. "This makes my day."

John picked me up, squeezing me tight against him. "What you do to me." He slid his hand up the back of my coat, resting his hands on my shoulder blades. I wriggled out of my coat and kissed him hungrily. I wanted to touch him, make out.

John slipped his hands under my sweater.

"Your fingers are freezing!" I cried.

"I'll warm them up on you," John said, pulling my sweater over my head. He fondled my skin, kissing me lightly. "You okay?"

I smiled, reaching for him. We got comfortable on the blanket, then I heard something. "What's that?" I sat up, terrified.

"It's raining," John said, caressing my shoulder. He pulled me back down. "No one will find us here, Margaret. We can do what we want."

My heart skipped. "Is that why you brought me here?" I sat up again, grabbing my sweater. "To monk me?"

"Well, yeah. I mean, no. I mean, isn't it time?" John stammered. "I thought . . ."

"You thought I'd be a floozie if we came here. I thought you were being romantic, you cared about me." I pulled my sweater back on. "Is sex all you want from me?" I screamed.

John grabbed me by the shoulders. "No, but I don't like being teased."

"I'm not teasing."

"Margaret, you act all hot, then you turn it off. What am I supposed to think?" John's voice grew louder. "You touch me, kiss me. Then you act all scared. I'm trying to understand."

"I'm not acting," I said quietly. "I *am* scared." I broke free from his grasp. "I want to touch you and kiss you. But what you want is a very big deal to me. I'm not like the others." I hugged myself.

John put his arms around me. He was breathing hard. His voice was husky. "I know you're not like the others. If you were anyone else, I'd be gone by now."

"I'm scared if I do this, you'll be done with me."

"What do I have to do to prove myself?"

"There are so many rumors about you."

"They're not true," John said.

"But you flirt with all the debs, even Dorothy," I cried. "I don't know what to believe."

John kissed me. "I'm sorry," he said. "I didn't know the flirting bothered you. It's just something I do."

I nodded. "Sometimes I don't know why you want me as a girlfriend."

John hugged me. We ate our picnic, talked, and kissed some more.

"I won't push any more, Margaret." He held my hand. "It's your decision—when, where. I've got the hots for you, and I don't want to be a knucklehead."

The next day at school, Dorothy approached us at the front door.

"Hi, devil," she winked.

"Dot," John said quietly. "Margaret's my baby, you know that, don't you?"

Dorothy's mouth hung open.

"Nobody else." John spun me around and walked me to my first class.

By February 6, I dreaded the morning *Gazette*. Justice department sources disclosed possible legislation that would permit "protective custody" arrest of any citizen for the duration of the war. Though the bill would be aimed solely at the dual citizenship problem of West Coast Japanese, it would also permit the seizure of any citizen in defense areas who could be considered dangerous to national security.

I jotted down the facts in my notebook, then reread them. I swallowed hard. I laid my notebook flat on the kitchen table and stared at the words.

"This is frightening," I said. "The Justice Department can only order the evacuation of enemy aliens from prohibited areas. If responsibility falls to the War Department, martial law could be declared in California."

"Please explain," Mother said, sitting down beside me.

"They could evacuate anyone, for any reason."

I read further in the *Gazette*:

Because Japanese aliens can not hold land in California, many have gained control of land by registering it in their children's names.

"That's what you did," I said.

"Yes," Father explained. "This way, we may work the land. And when I am gone, it will be for you children."

"But the government and other people don't see it that way. They think you're getting around the immigration laws."

"How can owning a few acres of land possibly be a threat to as great a country as this? I pay taxes each year on the land and income."

"I have a bad feeling about all of this."

"I only want to provide for my family and pass to my children the land I worked."

"Now white farmers want land the Issei have turned into precious farmland." I pointed to a quote in the paper by a spokesman for the white farmers:

People are saying we want the Japs to leave. We do. If all the Japs were rounded up and locked away forever, we'd never miss them. White farmers can produce anything the Japs can. They better not come back either.

I folded the *Gazette*, closed my notebook, and looked out the kitchen window. It would soon be spring, time for the crops.

CHAPTER 12
Executive Order 9066

On February 16, the *Gazette* had dreadful news. The California Joint Immigration Committee wanted all Japanese Americans removed from the Pacific Coast or any other "vital areas."

"Anyone who has Japanese blood must leave?" Mother asked over breakfast.

"That's what it sounds like. It says that 2,192 Japanese Americans are under arrest by the FBI," I explained.

"So many?" Mother said softly.

She was caught between cultures. She was raised in Japan, in a society where females are not considered as worthy as males. She tried very hard to adapt to American ways. My parents never bowed or spoke Japanese anymore, and they had mastered English. My mother had always been quiet. But since the bombing of Pearl Harbor, she had grown more vocal. She asked me to explain things from the paper. I discovered a different person within my mother.

The back door rattled, and John hollered, "Ready to go?"

Mother opened the door. "Good morning, John Wilson. Please have juice."

"Morning, Mrs. Yamaguchi. I've already eaten breakfast, but thank you."

I grabbed my jacket, pecking Mother's cheek. John snatched my books for me. Ever since our afternoon in the farm house, John had been more dreamy than ever. We still necked, but he never pushed to go further than I wanted. I was torn. I wanted to make out, but felt guilty. What would my mother think of me? We walked around to the front and began our trek to school.

"You kiddies have a good day today, you hear?" Mrs. Jenkins called.

Mr. Dennis spit on the ground. Mrs. Anderson yelled, "Dirty yellows!" All along the block, our neighbors turned their backs to us.

"Mrs. Jenkins is the only person I've babysat for since Christmas," I admitted.

"The neighbors haven't been talking to us as much either."

"Are your parents mad?"

"They adore you, Margaret. Our neighbors are drips."

"Nancy's devastated. She can't stand for people to treat her like an outcast."

John agreed. "She looks like she hasn't slept in days."

"At least she and Robert have each other."

"And us." John squeezed my hand.

"I'm sorry your life is being affected." I squeezed John's hand back.

"I couldn't stand not to have you in my life."

"It feels like a battlefield anywhere but home," I sighed.

"It's hooey," John said. "You're no different than you were three months ago."

"But the country is different," I pointed out.

The next day, I spotted posters on the way to school. They warned all enemy aliens they had one day to clear out of the prohibited areas. I stopped at the corner, glaring at the piece of paper.

"My father has to get permission to drive to his own orchard."

John put his arm around me and let me vent.

"How can this be happening?" I clenched my fists. "I'm just a regular deb. Because my parents are from Japan, my entire world is being torn apart."

"I'd change it if I could," he said.

I put my head into his shoulder. "We'd better get to school."

At school, things were even worse.

"Hey, slant eyes, why don't you go back to Japan?"

"You don't belong here, gookie."

"What are you doing, spying?"

There were only a handful of Japanese American students left in the high school. Most dropped out rather than face the hostility. I wanted to, because it would be easier than fighting. But after seeing Elizabeth try so hard to be my friend, I decided I wouldn't. This was my school too.

Some of the worst moments were when John and I were together.

One day at lunch, Daniel Rogers called, "Why don't you go with one of *our* girls, John. Mary Smith will be your squeeze. Don't waste your time with that little Jap."

My head whipped around. My mouth dropped open, and I felt the color drain out of my face. I pushed my fingernails into the palm of my hand as I tensed up.

John stared at Daniel as he squeezed my hand. "Margaret is *my* baby."

"She must do the cuzzy for you."

I started to shake my head. My body went rigid. I wanted to go home.

John stood up, his face purple. "Amscray!"

Daniel laughed and returned to his group of friends. I put my trembling hand on John's. He grabbed it and kissed my fingers.

"I'm sorry, Margaret."

"How could he say that?" I asked, fighting back tears. "He was my friend. He was at my birthday party."

"He's being a goon, like the rest of that group."

"Do they really think that's the only reason you'd be with me?" I asked softly.

"I don't care what they think," John said. "We know it's not true." John put my hand to his lips and held it there.

"Why don't you just stay away from me at school?" I suggested quietly.

"Are you dumping me?" John asked.

I shook my head. "I don't want you to get into fights. Maybe I *should* drop out of school."

"Then those knuckleheads would win." John held my hands between his. "Don't ever believe what the kids are batting their gums about."

"I don't." I shrugged. "I just wonder if it would be easier for everyone."

"This whole situation is all wet."

"I'm the enemy, and I haven't done anything wrong."

John and I walked past stores with signs in them that read "No Japs" and "Japs Go Home." I saw one window with a sign that said "Chinese American store."

My chest felt heavy. I couldn't endure any more horrible things inside me. John escorted me home and came in for cookies.

"I can't believe any of this is really happening," I said.

"All we should be worrying about is getting caught in the backseat of the car."

"Shhh," I whispered and smiled.

John ate three chocolate chip cookies and chugged a glass of milk. When he set his glass down, his upper lip was dripping with moo juice. Before I had time to say anything, he leaned toward me, kissed me, and left most of the milk on my mouth.

"John!" I squealed.

He dabbed my mouth with his napkin, then kissed me again.

"That's better."

February 19, 1942, was a turning point for the country and for my family. President Roosevelt signed Executive Order 9066, which authorized the secretary of war to define military areas "from which any or all persons may be excluded as deemed necessary or desirable."

"What does that mean, Margaret?" Mother asked.

"The War Department has the right to remove anyone, citizen or not, if they feel that person might be a threat to the war effort."

"What makes someone a threat?" Mother asked.

"This is such a vague order," I said. "It doesn't define a threat."

"We are not a threat," Father said. "The situation will soon return to normal."

"School will get better when the kids know *I'm* not a threat."

"Many Caucasians are fearful of any enemy aliens," Father said. "Talk of people leaving their homes is only fear. Neighbors will see we are not the enemy."

"Aren't all Americans actually aliens?" I grabbed my notebook. "The only true natives are the Indians, and they were ousted by the Europeans. Is the issue looking European versus looking like the enemy?"

As I thought about ancestry and native citizenship, I glanced at the rest of the article. The *Gazette* quoted Congressman Rankin of Missouri:

> *Once a Jap, always a Jap. I'm for taking every Japanese . . .*
> *and putting him in a concentration camp.*

"This guy is serious," I said, feeling the hair on the back of my neck stand up.

Father shook his head. "America would never do that. This man is hysterical."

"He's not alone. Another congressman from California said: 'We take cameras, guns, and radio sets from alien Japanese, but we don't take away cameras, guns, and radio sets from their children who are American citizens. The only solution . . .

is to remove from the area completely those persons who are likely to commit sabotage.'"

"We are safe," Father said. "We will not sabotage this country we love."

On February 20, General John Dewitt was appointed by the secretary of war to carry out Executive Order 9066. It was reported further evacuation could follow. Martial law was proposed, as was "protective custody" arrests of citizens and aliens.

I ran to the Wilsons. "John, my family might have to move away from the Coast!"

"That won't happen, Margaret. You haven't done anything wrong."

That day at school, Mrs. Grady spoke to me in private. "I have some bad news."

"I'm off the paper, aren't I?"

"I'm fighting every faculty member." Mrs. Grady embraced me tightly.

I staggered out of the journalism room, numb to my surroundings. I stumbled home and crawled into bed.

"Margaret?" Mother entered my room. "What is wrong, Daughter?"

"I'm off the paper."

She rocked me like I was a little girl. She pulled the covers around me and brought me tea. I started heaving. I couldn't stop. I lost five pounds by Saturday evening. I shoved my notebook in the corner of my closet, vowing to forget about it.

The next week, I didn't care about anything.

"I can't go to school again," I said, sitting at the table in my pajamas.

"You must," Father said.

"You will feel better when you are dressed," Mother said, ushering me upstairs. I sat on my bed as she dressed me.

John dragged me to school in the mornings. I went through my classes, oblivious to taunts. He guided me home after school, nestling with me, allowing me to mourn the loss of the *Sentinel.*

I was stunned when I read the *Gazette* on the twenty-sixth of February. The navy ordered Japanese American residents of Terminal Island, San Pedro, California, to leave within forty-eight hours, to settle wherever they could.

"Forty-eight hours?" Father said, looking confused. "This is not right."

For the first time, Father sounded doubtful. My blue mood deepened.

On the twenty-eighth, people talked about fifth column activity.

"What is that?" Mother asked.

Father looked at me for the answer.

"When people help the enemy from within their own country. Like a spy," I explained uneasily. I wanted my father to answer the questions, but he looked uncertain. "Even some Japanese American leaders in the JACL are saying Japanese should leave the Coast. This is bushwa. They have to have some proof of spying before they make anyone leave, don't they?"

"After they check out those they fear, people will return to their homes and lives." Father clung to his American beliefs, but his voice sounded unsure.

It frightened me to hear my father's doubt. He had always been the one to solve the problems. Fear crept through my chest.

"Why are these orders necessary?" I asked. "The government doesn't have proof of any spying." I ran upstairs and clawed through my closet. I grabbed my notebook for the first time in a week.

They're destroying people's lives without just cause. Father has no answer for me. I have to give a damn if my family is going to survive. I'm going to keep a record of what's happening. I want my family back to normal! I can't share my writing in the VV Sentinel, which breaks my heart, but I have a mission: to write.

I wrote down all the things that had happened since Pearl Harbor was attacked: the hateful words kids called me, love I felt for John, and my confusion.

I wrote for a solid hour before I put down my pen. I felt as if my body was cleansed. My thoughts seemed clearer than they had been all week. I looked in the mirror, horrified. My hair was stringy and hanging into my face. My face looked gray, with heavy dark circles under my eyes. After a long bath, I felt more alive, like I had washed away some of my troubles.

CHAPTER 13
Military Areas One and Two

Dear Diary,

I'm stronger than I realized. I have to be. My family needs me to be strong. I know now writing is an integral part of my existence. I feel so much better getting my thoughts onto paper. I'll chronicle our lives until this mess is straightened out. Maybe someday someone will want to read my words. Mostly, it's for me. I have to feel like I'm doing something. By writing down what happens to us, maybe I can do something. The school paper doesn't want me any longer. I'll find some other outlet.

I spent Saturday morning writing and eating. I was starved! John came over in the afternoon. "Why didn't you tell me how sub zero I looked all week?"

"You didn't look sub zero to me." John smoothed the hair out of my eyes.

"I was such a sad sack all week, everyone at school is probably *really* wondering why you're with me."

"I know *I* am," Timmy piped up. "You're a mess, Margaret."

I threw a sofa cushion at Timmy. "Go chase yourself."

"Hey, John," Timmy said, ignoring me. "I've been practicing my shots. Come outside with me." Timmy dragged John out to the basketball hoop. I watched out the window and felt strangely happy. If the world could be just as big as my backyard, I'd be happy forever. I joined them, practicing my own moves.

On March 2, 1942, Public Proclamation Number One was issued by General DeWitt. It designated the western halves of California, Oregon, Washington, and the southern part of Arizona as military area number one. Under the proclamation, Japanese, German, and Italian aliens and anyone of Japanese ancestry could be removed. The area was divided into two zones, A1 and B1. Enemy aliens were completely barred from zone A1. In zone B1, their movements were greatly restricted.

DeWitt would continue the evacuation process, ordering Japanese aliens and American-born Japanese to leave certain points in the future. The evacuation was reported to be for national security reasons, to protect the country from spies.

"Where would people go?" Mother asked.

"I don't know," I said. "But why are only the German and Italian *aliens* affected? If anyone with Japanese ancestry can be removed, why can't anyone with German or Italian ancestry also be removed?"

"What is the difference?"

"The government defines aliens as those born in another country. You and Father are considered aliens."

"But you are not an alien?" Father asked.

I stared at him. He knew I wasn't considered an alien. "No, but I have Japanese ancestry, so I'm affected."

"Would that not be much harder to accomplish?" Father asked.

I nodded, feeling a sense of betrayal. "What's eating me is Joe Regalatto's parents were born in Italy; he was born here. But only his parents are going to be affected. He isn't."

I read more from the paper. "This DeWitt says all Japanese—alien and American-born—should get out of Military

Area No. 1 now. Those that move to the interior probably won't be bothered again. Do you think we should go?"

"This is our home," Father said. "I must tend to my orchard."

"We have to do something. We can't just wait to be lynched."

Father walked out the back door.

By March 4, it became clear my family would be affected.

"This cannot happen, Margaret. You will see." Father went quietly about his normal routine, but his eyes looked worried. Many Japanese families in the county decided to leave, whether they were citizens or aliens. Some had been threatened by whites. Some had been beaten up. Goons circled the neighborhood. I knew several kids at school whose families had been attacked.

During the next week, my father started losing business orders. Some of his oldest customers called and canceled their standing orders. He took each phone call calmly, thanking the person for letting him know.

"What are you going to do?" I asked.

"We will sell our fruit." Father's voice cracked as he spoke. I realized he was trying hard to remain strong for his family. I saw him clench his teeth as the phone rang again.

I wanted to scream and tear somebody's eyes out. I put my arms around my father as he hung up the telephone. "I'm sorry."

Father nodded, but his eyes teared up. He and Uncle Hirato had nurtured their orchard from nothing into a productive, beautiful piece of land. Now, my father's dream was being rubbed out.

"Isn't there anything else we can do?" I asked angrily.

Father shook his head. "I do not know what, Margaret."

As I stood by the window and held my father's hand, a creeping anger started in my stomach. "Are you just going to give up?"

"I am not giving up," Father said shakily. He looked hurt. "I am trying to be a good citizen and do what is asked of me."

I dropped his hand. "This isn't right, Father. The government isn't going to take care of us. They don't want us here. Can't you see that?"

My father put his head down and refused to look at me. I left for school all balled up. I had never yelled at my father before and was sick to my stomach by first period. I didn't like the shift in our familial positions.

That day at school, we had a surprise math quiz.

"Mr. Peterson pulled a Jap on us," Mary Smith moaned.

I answered every question, turned in my test, and left school.

In the evenings, Nancy, Robert, John, and I kept company in our basement. Timmy snuck down. We were too tired to chase him away, so he played with Trixie while we tried to make sense of our changing world and snuck in some necking. It was cozy, and for a couple of hours we forgot about the madness the war was heaping on our lives. School had become so intense, all four of us were exhausted by the end of each day.

"I don't know if I can keep going to school," Nancy said.

"You'd drop out?" I asked.

"I have to struggle in every class, and it just doesn't seem worth it." Tears welled up in her eyes.

"I'm struggling now, too, Nancy. The teachers aren't grading us fairly." I thought about what she said. Mr. Peterson had deliberately failed me on the test, even though I knew my answers were correct. I grabbed Nancy's hands. "You've always stood up for yourself." I put my head down. "I've wanted to quit for weeks, but kept going because of the three of you," I said quietly. "I hate confrontation."

"I'll hate it if you three leave school," John said.

The *Gazette* was filled with more unsettling news every day. Enemy aliens were classified for greater efficiency. A progressive evacuation of the five classes of aliens and citizens followed:

1. Those suspected of sabotage or subversive activity.

2. Japanese aliens.

3. Japanese Americans

4. German aliens

5. Italian aliens.

After the military areas are cleared of Japanese, German and Italian aliens would follow. German and Italian aliens over the age of 70 will only be required to move if individually suspected. German and Italian aliens who had children in the armed forces of the United States probably won't be required to move.

"Horsefeathers!" I said. "Why aren't the German and Italian aliens treated the same as Japanese? They're singling out one race."

As more Japanese American families in the county and the state were affected, panic set in. Many local families felt pressured to sell their homes and land for a fraction of their worth. Mrs. Sato had been bullied into selling her family's car for twenty dollars.

"Margaret, it was loathsome," Nancy said. "This goon from down the street threatened to let my mom have it if she didn't sell him the hayburner."

"Jeepers, what did your dad say?" I asked.

"He told her not to open the door again unless it was someone we knew."

"Someone came to our door and wanted to look around inside, to go through our things, as if we were having some kind of yard sale," I said.

"What did you do?" Nancy asked.

"My father wouldn't let them in, but three men forced their way into our house, breaking my mother's lamp. Mr. Wilson and John were over, so they said they had already purchased everything."

"The Wilsons are so darb!" Nancy cried. "You were lucky!"

"We aren't going to open the door anymore either." I looked at Nancy. "It gives me the heebie-jeebies to think what those men might have done." Nancy was right. John was a darb! Had I been overlooking that lately?

By March 9, the *Gazette* urged the Japanese to stop selling. Aliens tempted to get rid of possessions were told to work their land until positive they would be leaving.

Thoughts of leaving school and possibly California overwhelmed me as I walked home from school that day. In the afternoon light, the streets seemed grayer than I ever remembered. I wondered where the color had gone.

CHAPTER 14
Public Proclamations and Private Battles

On March 12, 1942, the secretary of the treasury designated the Federal Reserve Bank as the authority handling Japanese American property.

"The government is looking out for us." Father smiled.

"Dig this," I said. "In order to store personal property with the Federal Reserve Bank, evictees are required to sign a form."

"What kind of form?" Father asked.

"It says the Federal Reserve Bank has no liability or responsibility for what happens to property."

"Does that mean they will not insure our possessions?"

"It's a bunch of hooey." I shook my head. "There's no insurance on anything left with the Federal Reserve Bank."

"What do we do?" Father sounded small, like a chunk of his resolve had broken away.

"The bank is encouraging people to liquidate their property." I touched my father's hands. "In other words, get what you can for your land."

"Would you trust them?"

"No." Fear spread in my stomach. I wanted him to be the old father again.

Father grabbed my fingers and closed his eyes. Then he walked out of the kitchen to his truck. I watched as he drove toward his orchard, the land he loved more than anything except his family.

I read further in the paper and shook my head. Japanese American farms were to be transferred to Caucasian tenants and corporations. Farms would be transferred back after the war. Japanese American farmers were told to continue farming activities in the time before eviction. Destruction of crops would be punished as sabotage.

I hopped on my bike and rode to the orchard. I was so angry, I felt like I could ride forever. I concentrated on the narrow road, the trees. As I approached the orchard, it erupted into view. Vibrant colors exploded from the trees, and the air was saturated with fruity smells. I stood at the entrance to the orchard and marveled at the beauty of the place. Twenty years before, it had been abandoned as worthless. Now, flowers and fruits grew everywhere.

I watched my father labor over the fruits he grew. He and Uncle Toshio toiled very hard, but they enjoyed the work. Tears sprang to my eyes as I thought about him leaving all this. "For crying out loud," I said to myself. "What threat is he to anyone?"

Father tenderly weeded and watered, all the while smiling. It seemed as if the worries, the doubts, and the years were erased from his face. I suddenly knew why he wanted to believe so hard in America. He came to this country to live a dream. And now, his dreams were being loused up, just because he was born in Japan. I didn't agree with his blind faith, but I understood him a bit more.

On Sunday afternoon, I told John, "I don't know what we'll do without any money coming in."

"Don't your folks have any saved up?"

"There's a limit to how much of their own money they can withdraw each month." I put my head down. "We've spent all we can for this month already. I don't know how we're going to get by."

On March 16, DeWitt issued Public Proclamation Number Two, creating military areas in Idaho, Montana, Nevada, and Utah.

Mother came to me with the newspaper. "I am confused."

"It means there are more restrictions, more places we can't go." I bit my lip. "We can't go in certain zones in eight states now. They keep saying to move to the interior of the United States. I want to go," I pleaded.

"We must listen to Father."

"What if he's wrong?"

Mother said nothing.

That day, I was called to the principal's office. Was I being booted out of school? When I walked in, Robert and John were sitting on the chairs beside the secretary. Robert's eyes were swollen, his upper lip cracked and bleeding. It looked like he had a broken nose. He was listing to the side, leaning on John.

"What happened to you two?" I knelt in front of Robert.

"Some of my *teammates* cornered me in the locker room," Robert said.

"They beat you up?" I asked.

"Gave me the business."

"Have you seen a doctor?"

"The nurse told me to wait."

"They could have killed you," I said.

"They almost did," John said.

"They've got a lot of moxie!" I said indignantly. "What did the principal say?"

"As far as he's concerned, what we say is jive," John said.

"If John hadn't come looking for me, they'd probably still be working me over," Robert said softly, looking around the office. "I owe him my life."

"For crying out loud!" My anger overtook my fear and sadness. I grabbed Robert's hands. "I'll call Mother."

"I called my mom, Margaret," John said. "Since your mom doesn't drive, I figured mine could take Robert to the doctor."

John's hands were bruised. He had a cut above one eye. "Just had to be a he-man, huh?" I grazed his cheek with my fingers.

"Robert's being blamed for the fight," John snarled.

"You're off your nuts, you know that?" As I stared at John, an overwhelming feeling of love filled me. I did the only thing I could—I kissed his bruised knuckles.

Robert leaned over, so his mouth was at my ear. "They called him a three-letter man, Mar."

"Because he helped you?"

John laughed. "Let them call me a F-A-G. Maybe they'll leave Margaret alone."

I caressed John's knee.

That afternoon, Timmy was frantic. "Is Robert going to die?" he sobbed.

"No," I said. "He's going to need some time to heal up."

Timmy hugged me hard and cried. I patted his back and tried to comfort him. After his sobs turned to hiccups, he curled up on the floor in Robert's room.

Mother's face was strained. "I cannot believe his friends would do this to him."

"They have been tainted by the ugliness of the war," Father said.

"If John hadn't been there, they might have killed Robert," I said quietly. "And now, both John and Robert are left holding the bag. John and his parents are different from what you feared, Mother."

"I am glad." Mother embraced me.

I let a few tears slide down my cheek before I choked back my emotions. "Now he's labeled as a traitor and a homosexual by those boys."

Nancy and John came over after dinner. While Robert slept, we talked.

"Besides the obvious injuries to his face, his ribs are bruised, they broke his little finger and his nose, and he was kicked hard enough in the back to cause some internal bleeding," I admitted, shaking as I spoke.

"Is he really okay?" Nancy asked, crying.

"He'll be all right. But I'm afraid for all of us now. Those boys would have killed him if John hadn't walked in. And now that John got in a fight *defending* Robert, he's going to be harassed even more."

"I can take care of myself," John said. His face was puffy and purple, and his hands were swollen.

"What if they gang up on you?" I asked, kissing his knuckles. "I think you should stay away from me at school."

"I don't want to."

"Maybe it would be better for all four of us. The situation is getting dangerous."

"Maybe." John held my hand. "But I don't like it."

That night, after Nancy went home, I planted butterfly kisses on John's face, starting at his eyebrows, his nose, his lips.

"Hot dog!" he said. "What's that for?"

"You've proven yourself," I said softly, my heart ready to explode. I slipped my dress off, letting it slide to the floor. I stood before him in my slip.

"Your parents . . . ," John said.

I placed my finger on his lips. "This isn't as romantic as the farm house, but . . ." I sat on his lap, kissing him. I didn't worry about anything. I felt no shame. His hands touched me. His lips kissed me. He wrestled my slip over my shoulders. I shimmied out of my bra and panties and watched him gaze at me.

"Exquisite," he whispered.

I helped him out of his clothes, and we made love on the basement floor. He touched me gently, as if I might break.

"Margaret," John breathed. "I love you."

We held each other. "I love you, too, John Wilson."

On March 18, President Roosevelt created the War Relocation Authority (WRA). Milton Eisenhower was named director. He was responsible for a plan to remove designated persons from the restricted areas.

"How will they determine designated persons?" Father asked anxiously.

"It doesn't say." I frowned.

On March 20, Japanese Americans were advised by the army to settle their affairs and prepare to move, although no formal evacuation was planned. DeWitt wanted to give aliens a fair chance to prove their loyalty to the United States.

"He will give us a chance to prove loyalty," Father said. "That will settle things."

"How?" I slammed the paper down. "They're telling everyone who looks Japanese to leave." I felt disgusted with Father's naive faith.

The next day, horror shook my body as I read the *Gazette*'s top story:

Manzanar opens in California, the first assembly center
for evacuated Japanese Americans.

"Father, this is real. It's happening." I pointed to the article.

"It is not here," Father said.

"We could end up in a place just like it!" I shouted. "Just yesterday, they wanted to give the Japanese a chance to prove their loyalty. So why is an assembly center opening today? What about proof of loyalty?"

My father looked confused. I forced my father to look at me. "The government is moving people, against their will, into camps. I want us to leave now while we can."

CHAPTER 15
To Stay or Leave?

On March 24, Public Proclamation Number Three was issued. DeWitt established curfew and travel regulations for Japanese, German, and Italian aliens and Japanese Americans. Those Japanese considered enemy aliens and American-born Japanese had to obey travel restrictions, curfew, and contraband regulations.

"It should affect American born Germans and Italians also," I protested.

Mother looked at me.

"It's because we're easy to spot." I stumbled to my room. For the first time in my life, I felt different from my neighbors. I gaped into the mirror and instead of seeing Margaret Yamaguchi, a Japanese face stared back at me. Who was I?

"It doesn't matter that I was born here," I said to John on the way to school. "They only see the enemy." I caught my breath.

John tugged me close. "I love you, no matter what other people see."

I clutched him. What would I do without him?

On March 26, the paper reported an end to the voluntary evacuation of Japanese and Japanese Americans along the

Pacific Coast. General DeWitt signed Public Proclamation Number Four, giving Japanese aliens until March 28 to leave. After then, they would be evacuated under army supervision.

"I do not understand this," Mother said.

"They've been encouraging the Japanese to leave," I snarled. "All of a sudden, they want the Japanese to stay put."

"There are only two more days to leave," Father said quietly. His eyes drooped.

"What will we do, Father?"

"What would *you* do, Margaret?"

I swallowed. "We should go."

He closed his eyes. "I must stay and tend our crops."

"What about Uncle Toshio?"

"He will take his family inland."

I glared at my father. "They're leaving, and we're staying?"

Father nodded. "We must help them pack and prepare them for their journey."

"Where are they going?"

"I do not know. God will be with them."

"Why aren't we going too?" I tried to control my voice, but couldn't breathe.

"We have no place to go."

"Neither do they!" I shouted. "We're going to be trapped here. Can't you see what's happening?"

"I cannot abandon our orchard."

"Can you honestly do all the work alone?" I stared at my father. "It's always been you and Uncle Toshio."

"I will do what I am able."

"How can he leave without us?"

"He feels strongly in his decision. I feel strongly in mine."

"You've always taught us we should stick together, as a family. We should leave with them."

"We must have faith, Margaret."

"In what? This government doesn't want you!"

"I have made our decision," Father said softly. He wouldn't look at me.

"It's the wrong decision!" I stormed out of the kitchen. I felt out of control but justified. We needed to stand up for ourselves.

We helped my uncle's family pack all weekend, along with the Wilsons. Barbara was waddling now, and tried to help, but had to rest often. It seemed like the accumulation of everything was visible on her face—sleeplessness, fear, and anger.

"Why don't you go with them?" I asked her. "You and Howard could go with Uncle Toshio, and you wouldn't have to be in this mess."

"We talked about it, Margaret, but we couldn't leave the family behind. We'll be okay, if we stay together."

I didn't believe that. Not totally. I thought my sister and her husband should leave with our uncle. At least she'd be with family, and Aunt Aiko could help with the baby. But she and Howard stayed.

When the truck and car were packed to overflowing, we had a family feast.

"I'm going to miss you, Dorothy," I said, sitting next to my cousin. "I wish we were going with you."

"There's no guarantee we'll be safe if we leave, but we know for sure it isn't good to stay." She looked down. "There's no way to convince your father?"

I shook my head and pulled Dorothy into the kitchen. "I don't agree with him, but what can I do?"

"Come with us!" Dorothy pleaded.

"Could you abandon your parents?"

We sent Uncle Toshio and his family on their way early Sunday morning. I cried, hoping I would see them again, afraid for them and for us. I wanted to leave with them, knowing we were stuck in California. I felt powerless and panicked.

They called from Denver. When they reached the California border, they had to have a destination, or they would have been turned back. Steven opened up the Denver phone book, picked out a name, and called it. Steven told the man their plight, and asked if they could give their name as a destination. The man said yes.

"Thank goodness they found people willing to help," I said.

"Give thanks to God for their safe arrival," Father said.

"We should have left with them." I went to my room to write in my diary.

> *I am the most frightened I have ever been. Without Uncle Toshio's family here with us, I feel like we're weaker. Father was wrong. We should have left. At least leaving gave us a chance. But now, we're at the mercy of those who already hate us. What's going to happen to us? What's the matter with him? He's such a patsy, believing in this government. I feel vulnerable, like we're all alone now. Father won't listen to me, and I'm so angry with him.*

The next week at school, some of the other Asian kids wore buttons. As I walked by, I noticed they said "Chinese" or "Not from Nippon." Some kids hissed at me. I found a dead pig in my locker.

I screamed, threw my books inside and ran to the principal's office.

"There's a dead pig in my locker," I said at the counter.

The secretary sneered at me. "So? What do you want me to do about it?"

"Find out who put it there."

"Did you see anyone put it in there?"

"No."

"Then why are you accusing someone of doing it?"

I clenched my teeth. "Can you at least get a janitor to take it away?"

"Mr. Black is cleaning the halls right now. You'll have to wait until after lunch."

"But it will stink by then."

The secretary ignored me and returned to her typing.

"What a rotten double-crossing . . . ," I muttered as I marched back to my locker. I opened the door, holding my nose. I ran to the girls' lavatory and grabbed a fist full of papers towels, then quickly lifted the pig out of the bottom of my locker.

Nancy scooted over to me. "Lamb pie, what is that?"

"Someone put this in my locker."

"Ugh! They got that biology juice all over everything."

I threw the pig into the garbage with a thud and washed my hands, but my clothes stunk all day of formaldehyde. The more I thought about it, the more I fumed.

My only sanctuary in the school had been the journalism room. School used to bring me joy, now it was a nightmare. I had no safe place to go. Walking between classes was dangerous. Several times, boys had stopped me in the hall and threatened me. The worst incident happened outside the principal's office.

"Boing!" a chorus of male voices rang out.

A couple of senior boys approached me. One stepped in front of me and one stepped behind me.

"Hey, Jap hot cake," one said. "Leave our kind alone. Get yourself a Jap boy."

I tried to go around him. The other boy grabbed my arm and twisted me around.

"You're poison."

The principal's office door was open. I knew the secretary could hear.

"Maybe we should see if she's worth it. Must be a goo ball, if John's with her."

"Come on," the first one said, squeezing my arm. "He won't mind sharing."

"We know you've let him, now let us."

They jerked me toward the boys' restroom. Terror raced through my body. I screamed, trying to yank myself free. I kicked and bit at them. They slapped me.

"What is going on?" Mrs. Grady boomed as she rounded the corner. She grabbed a fistful of one boy's hair, but the others got away.

"Go inside, Margaret," she said gently.

I held my stinging cheek and slunk into the office.

Mrs. Grady hauled the boy into the office. "What is wrong with you, Madeline?" Mrs. Grady screamed. "Couldn't you hear what was going on out there?"

"I thought they were just playing around. You know how those Jap girls are."

The boy snickered.

"I'm reporting this boy. And I'll report you the next time you ignore a student, Madeline."

"Can't prove a thing," the boy snarled. "Sticking up for your brown-nosing Jap."

Mrs. Grady stuck her face in his. "Don't push me."

"You want to keep your job, back off, pinko."

"You're in my senior English, aren't you, Mr. Davis?"

The boy nodded.

"You need that to graduate, don't you?"

The boy's mouth dropped open. "You wouldn't dare."

"If you or any of your buddies come near Margaret again, I will fail you." She hustled me out of the office.

"Thank you, Mrs. Grady." I stepped into the restroom and splashed my face with cold water. "It gives me the heebie-jeebies to think what they would have done."

"I'll escort you to classes today, dear."

By the end of March, school had become so potentially violent that Robert, Nancy, and I quit. I felt like I had lost a battle. But I knew if we continued going, we were going to be seriously hurt. My parents pulled Timmy out of school.

After I left school, John didn't have as much trouble with his classmates. I saw him after school. I knew I could ultimately win the war. I wasn't giving up, even if the battles were getting tougher.

"Tell them we broke up," I said to John.

Every afternoon John went home for dinner, then came to our house through the backyards. Mrs. Jenkins didn't mind. He brought his homework and stayed until bedtime. Our families accepted this, knowing our lives were about to change.

One afternoon, I was sitting on our front steps, waiting for John to come home. I spotted him strolling down the street with Mary Smith! She had her arm draped through his and her head resting on his shoulder. My heart rolled. I scooted into the house, peeking out the front window. Mary pecked his cheek. As soon as she was out of sight, I phoned John.

"What's going on?" I demanded.

"What do you mean?" John said.

"Why were you walking home with Mary Smith?"

"She walked with me, Margaret. I didn't invite her."

"It didn't look like you tried very hard to get away."

"They think I dumped you. I have to play the part."

"It looked pretty authentic." I hung up.

All that night, I wouldn't come to the phone or the front door to talk to John. My heart was broken. If he wanted to spoon with Mary, let him.

Dear Diary,

How stupid I was to trust him. I thought he truly loved me. I guess I was wrong. He got what he wanted. He probably bragged to all the boys at school and told them how he talked me into it. Stupid!

That night, Robert knocked on my bedroom door. "Can I come in, Mar?"

"It's open."

He sat on the edge of my bed and rubbed my shoulder. "I heard about Mary."

"Why did he do that to me, Robert? I thought he loved me."

"He does. I know what it looked like, but John's all busted up over this. I've been over there for the last two hours. Mar, he's going crazy."

"He let her kiss him!"

"It was foul." Robert sighed. "He's just a lunkhead."

"Did he do anything with her?" I asked softly.

"Holy Joe, no. She latched on to him after last class and wouldn't let go. You know how wild the girls are for him. They all figure he's back in play."

"I guess you're right."

"Go to the back door and see him?"

John stood in our yard with an armload of orchids. "Margaret," he said when I opened the door. He pulled me outside. "Mary is nothing to me." He handed me the orchids. "You're the only girl I want to be with. You're the only one I'm *with*."

"How can I believe you?"

"My class ring." John stepped toward me. "I've never given it to another deb."

"I guess I'm jealous," I said, sitting on the top step. "All those rumors I've heard about your being a wolf. And we did . . . Then, I saw you with her."

John scooted close and put his arms around me. "I can imagine how it looked. I'd tear some guy apart if I thought he was wolfing on you."

"I've done things with you I never thought I'd do until after I was married."

"Forgive me?" John put his head on my shoulder and batted his eyes at me.

I laughed so hard, tears ran down my face. "You're a nut." I pecked his cheek.

"Only for you." He put a flower in my hair, and we cuddled until dawn.

My father's decision to stay past March 28 had sealed our fate. I feared it was a decision we'd regret.

CHAPTER 16
The End?

April was humdrum. I spent my time writing and helping my mother. Barbara and Howard had moved into the basement, so she and I spent more and more time together talking. And of course, Timmy was underfoot.

I spilled my feelings onto the pages of my diary:

I'm so confused. What am I supposed to do? How am I supposed to think? I'm so bored without school. What do I do? And I miss John. Without my writing, I don't know what I'd fill my days with.

Robert and Nancy spent most of their time at Nancy's house, and I was lonely. I wandered around the house until John came home from school, then clung to him until he left. My writing sustained me through the daytime, and John made my life seem complete. We had to scratch up private moments; so when we did manage to be alone, it was extra luscious.

Robert yelled from his room one night. "What happened in here?"

Sheets were piled on the floor, and Trixie was using them as a bed.

"These were clean yesterday," Robert said.

"Calm down," I said. "Timmy did it."

"Why?"

"You used to take Timmy everywhere."

"You think he feels left out because I'm dating Nancy?" Robert asked.

John joined us for dinner, and Timmy scrambled to sit next to him. "John, show me how to do a lay-up," Timmy pleaded. "Please."

"Sure, Tiger." After dessert, John took Timmy to the back-yard hoop and spent two hours practicing lay-ups and free throws. I perched on the steps and sketched them. The look of joy on Timmy's face was priceless.

After Timmy went to bed, I said, "I appreciate your spend-ing time with the pest."

"Timmy's great," John grinned. "I have a lot of fun with him."

"Seriously? Or are you just doing this because of me?"

"Seriously." John put his arm around me. "I love you. And your family."

"Timmy's taking Robert and Nancy's dating so hard. I worry about him." I kissed John. "You're almost too good to be true."

On April 4, the *Valle Verde Gazette* reported:

The Salinas fairgrounds is one of six additional assembly centers for use in the evacuation of Japanese. Expected to accommodate 3,000, the grounds will be used only to collect aliens for transfer to reception centers, such as Manzanar.

"People will have to stay at the fairgrounds?" I said.

"There must be temporary shelter," Father said.

"This makes us sound like animals being shuttled from place to place."

On April 7, Milton Eisenhower, director of the WRA, asked the governors of ten western states to accept Japanese Ameri-can evacuees. Only Colorado Governor Ralph Carr offered cooperation.

"We aren't wanted anywhere," I told John after school.

"I want you here with me," John said, twirling me into his arms.

I spent the next two weeks packing up our household items and helping my mother in her flower garden. I enjoyed the sunshine and felt isolated in our backyard. My world was becoming smaller; it felt as if I were getting smaller. Some days I wanted to just disappear altogether, to ignore the problems in my life.

Dear Diary,

I hate the thought of leaving our things behind. Memories are wrapped up in our furniture, stuff in our house. I've walked through, running my hands over all of our material possessions. I have to take my record player and my typewriter. No matter what. I hate the thought of leaving John behind. Will he forget me when we leave?

I filled my notebook with descriptions and poems and sketches of our home and our life, like an observer, recording moments out of someone else's life.

On Tuesday, April 21, we knew what our fate would be. By the end of April, we would be in the Salinas fairgrounds. We would stay there until transferred to a relocation center. I dashed to meet John at the corner. "We have to report to the Veterans building on Saturday!"

He caught me in his arms, and I went limp. I felt my strength fading. My tenacity to be a fighter crumbled a bit. John helped me to the house, and we held each other while I explained, through sobs. "We have to live in the fairgrounds, John. How can this be happening?"

John smoothed my hair away from my face and rubbed my back.

"If we had just left when we could have . . . ," I said.

John kissed me. "Salinas is less than an hour away."

"What's going to happen to us?" I whispered.

"Whatever happens," John said. "I'll find a way to be with you."

My strength rebounded as we held each other. I had to face my fate with dignity or the pantywaisted government would win.

The next day, one of our neighbors started to plow under his field. He decided that if his crops were going to be abandoned, the government wasn't going to get the fruits of *his* labor. The cops pinched him for sabotage.

Father and I reported Saturday morning to the Veterans Building. We were given numbers, one for each of us in the family. We were given vague instructions about what to take: bedding and linens, extra clothes for all kinds of weather, toiletries, tableware and "essential personal effects," whatever that was. Each person had to carry their own luggage; there would be no assistance. We were told to return next Monday, April 27, for evacuation.

As we departed, a Caucasian man sobbed, "What about my wife?"

"You don't have to go, but your Jap wife and son do," said the clerk.

"What will I do?" the man asked.

"Forget them and move ahead with your life."

"I can't do that."

The *Gazette* had a notice in it to all Japanese subscribers:

Please notify the Valle Verde Gazette of your new address.
You will not be charged any extra for mail subscriptions
and can have the GAZETTE delivered wherever you go.

For the next three days, we sorted and packed, frantically deciding what to take and what to abandon.

"We can store your things," Mr. Wilson said. "We'll just stuff the basement as full as it will go."

"And the shed," Mrs. Wilson offered. "However we can help, we will."

"Thank you," my father said. "I am touched by your kindness."

We carted boxes and boxes from our house to theirs. We sorted through pictures and memories and mementos of our lives. We gave a lot away.

"Can I store anything for you?" Mrs. Jenkins asked as we carried a load to the Wilsons. "Or keep an eye on anything while you're gone."

Mother grabbed Mrs. Jenkins' hand. "You are generous."

"It's a crying shame this is happening," Mrs. Jenkins chanted. "Just a shame."

Most of the other Japanese American families in the county had no friends to help them. The Satos had to give away everything they couldn't store at Mrs. Jenkins'.

John helped me clean out my bedroom.

"I'm trying to memorize everything," I said, as I boxed up things from my dresser.

"Never figured I'd be alone in your room with you," John teased.

"I wish it were for some other reason."

"Are these antiques?"

"My bed, my dresser, and my vanity all came from my mother's family in Japan," I said. "They're very old and delicate."

"Let's move them first," John offered.

We were not told how or where to live, either at the assembly center or the more permanent relocation center. I packed my pearls I had received from John and my notebooks. They were my essentials.

"We can't take Trixie," I said.

"We have to," Timmy cried. "She'll miss us."

"The Wilsons will keep her for us." She was an old dog, and I knew she would die without us. But at least we had people we could trust.

After we emptied our house and transferred boxes to the Wilsons, they invited us over for a farewell dinner.

"I wish we could help you more," Mr. Wilson told my father. "I'll buy what I can from you. I'll definitely buy the house so you don't lose everything. Then I'll sell it back after this mess is straightened out."

"I thank you for your kindness," Father said. "You are a true friend."

"I'm so ashamed of our government," Mr. Wilson said. "There's nothing I can say or do that can begin to make up for what you're going through."

John and I slipped out to our backyard.

"I'll miss this house. I've always lived here." I put my head on his shoulder.

"I'm going to miss you," John said as he kissed me. He wrapped his arms around me, and I put my arms around his neck. "Margaret, I don't want to do this for the wrong reasons," he took a deep breath and leaned his forehead against mine.

"The only time I feel alive is when we're touching." I reached up and kissed him more. "Take me back to the farm house?"

"Now?" John asked.

"It's my last chance to see it."

We spent the night in the house, caressing each other until the morning.

On April 27, the evacuation began. That morning, I stepped out of our house, feeling like my body was going to pull apart. I almost wished it would, then I wouldn't have to deal with this agony. I touched our door and looked at the house I had always called home. My chest and throat burned with suppressed tears. When would I see it again?

The Wilsons drove us to the bus station, where Japanese Americans milled around, waiting to board the buses. I clenched John's hand. I saw ladies all dressed up in their finest clothes, just like my mother. They looked proud and sad. Some of the angriest men wore army uniforms. I couldn't blame them. They had served America in the armed forces and were now being carted off to an assembly center. Everyone wore a tag on their clothing, like we were pieces of baggage.

When it was our turn to board the bus, I kissed John again. I closed my eyes and thought if I just remained inside his arms and never opened my eyes again, they couldn't make me leave. But I had to get on the bus.

"We're going to follow you," John said.

My heart was breaking. I sat with Timmy and held his hand. The Satos left on the same bus, so Robert and Nancy sat together. Suddenly, I was jealous. Because they were both Japanese Americans, they would go through this ordeal together. Because John was Caucasian, I had to go through it without him. How would I do it? Army guards slammed the windows closed and dropped the shades.

"We can't even look out the window?" I asked.

The bus ride seemed to take forever. I closed my eyes. Every time I opened them, I thought the sides of the bus were caving in on me.

When we arrived at Salinas, I was shocked. Army men with guns stood everywhere. We registered at the armory and were given a number, our address for our new temporary home. I had assumed that they had built shelters, like my father said, but no shelters existed. After traipsing through barns, we finally found our new home.

"Stalls?" I cried. "We have to live in stalls? There are five of us." Each family was given one stall to live in. There were no beds, only straw bales, with which to make mattresses, sitting outside the stalls. Those mattresses would be the only thing between us and a dirt floor.

"It isn't even clean." Timmy held his nose.

The straw on the floor of the stall was left over from the last inhabitant—a race horse. John and his parents were horrified at the prospect of us living in a stall. We all pitched and scooped the filthy straw out of the stall with our hands and piled it at the corner of the building. After a long hour, the floor was fairly clean, but the stall still smelled like horse manure.

"I'll bring bleach tomorrow," Mrs. Wilson said. "And buckets to pack water."

"Hey, John," Timmy said. "Will you help me find the bathroom?"

I noticed several toilets set up near the entrance. No curtains, no stalls, just toilets in the open. I watched as some of the men walked into the grass to go to the bathroom. I felt trapped.

"Is that the only bathroom?" I said, pointing.

Everyone looked. John grabbed my hand. "There must be something else."

I felt so humiliated. Guards stood right in front of the toilets.

"They couldn't place them behind a building?" Mrs. Wilson said.

"What do we do?"

"What if we hold up blankets or form a body block?" John asked.

"I guess we'll have to."

Our little group walked toward the bathrooms. We each took turns standing around the one needing to use the toilet. Everyone faced outward and formed a circle to give a bit of privacy.

Trudging back to our stall, I couldn't stop the tears. "Where are Barbara and Howard?" I asked. "Has anyone seen them?"

"No," Mother said. "We have not located them yet."

That afternoon, we stuffed straw into the potato sacks, making our mattresses. John held the sack open while I crammed in as much straw as I could. I was tired, hungry, and scratched from the straw. I wanted to take a bath.

"Maybe we can make something out of this stuff," Timmy said, dumping a bunch of scrap lumber at the door to our stall.

"I can't keep my eyes open," I said when the stars came out.

"We'll be back tomorrow," John promised.

I kissed him, needing to taste him, touch him. As long as he was close, he was my reality.

CHAPTER 17
Life in a Horse Stall

The next day, I traipsed past the open bathroom, searching for an enclosed one. Other women did the same thing. At least the men could walk into the weeds and do their business.

I inched along the perimeter of the fence, noticing the guards on the towers. I stared at them, baffled at their guns. I felt like a prisoner.

"What are you doing?" one snarled at me.

"Why do you have guns?" I asked.

"For your protection."

As I tramped away, I muttered, "If it's for our protection, why are the guns pointing *at* us?" I *was* a prisoner!

I searched all morning and finally found Nancy.

"Margaret, lamb pie, I'm so glad you're here."

I hugged Nancy.

"I'm close to where Barbara and Howard are." Nancy hooked her arm through mine. "They're at the end of this row."

"At least we're here together," I said.

"I'd go crazy if you and Robert weren't here," Nancy said.

An hour later, I was feeling loathsome. Nancy and Robert wanted to neck.

"You don't mind, do you, lamb pie?" Nancy giggled.

I did mind, but I wasn't going to say so. I stomped back to our stall. "Timmy, want to walk with me?"

"You going over to Nancy's?"

"Nope."

Timmy and I marched around the camp. "Is John going to get here soon? What do you suppose he's doing? He sure is a good basketball player, isn't he?"

I nodded, letting Timmy chatter. When we stumbled onto Robert and Nancy in the weeds, Robert jumped up quickly.

"Hey, Timmy. Whatcha doing?"

"Why do you care?" Timmy mumbled and walked off. I followed him, ignoring Robert's and Nancy's calls.

During lunch, Timmy asked her, "Nancy, why aren't you eating with your own family. Why are you stealing my family?"

I looked at Nancy and Robert and didn't know what to say. I had to hide a smile.

There were lots of teenagers at Salinas, but most I didn't know. I was simply too shy to approach any of the debs.

The stall, our "home," was just big enough for us to lie down, side by side, at night. I had cried myself to sleep the previous night, thinking of my beautiful room in our house— my own bed with comfortable sheets. I never realized just how wonderful my life used to be.

As I changed my clothes, I noticed holes in the slats. Boys were watching me! I wanted to die. I waited for two hours before I came out and vowed to never do that again. I found rocks and pieces of broken scrap lumber and stuffed the holes shut. Anger rose up in me. It gave me the screaming meemies to think they saw me!

Dear Diary,

Is this what life is reduced to? Cowering in a horse stall, so creeps don't see my body. I want John to touch me, kiss me. I don't think I can make it through this without him. My skin feels too tight. I want to scream. I feel like an animal!

"We brought some fruit," John said when he and his parents arrived. He opened up a box of peaches, and I breathed in the sweet smell.

"The food here is awful," I said. "We have to eat in communal mess halls. We can't even cook for ourselves." I picked up a peach and ran it around my palm. "They've served a thin gruel, and the fruits and vegetables are actually rotting."

John held me. "I'm sorry. We'll bring something each day."

"You can come every day?"

"My mom wants to come every day until your mother is more settled." He handed me a plate wrapped in a towel. "Mrs. Jenkins sent cookies."

John and I cleaned the stall a second time, using bleach. Then we tacked up blankets his parents had brought to give ourselves a little bit of privacy. When we were finished, John and I trudged around the grounds. I noticed the guards glaring at us.

"Better watch your back, son," the guard said. "No telling what those Japs'll do."

"Stuff a sock in it," John said.

"Don't threaten me, boy," the guard said. "Or you won't see your precious quiff."

John's jaw clenched. I pulled him away from the guard, terrified. "Could he keep you from entering the camp?"

"We need permission to enter. And the guards can pretty much do as they like. If they're in a bad mood, they don't have to let us in."

"What's your reason for coming?" I asked.

"We have to have your folks go over some contracts on the house and a bunch of things we're *buying* from you."

Too soon, it was time for John to leave. "Will I see you tomorrow?" I asked.

"As soon as I can get here."

I felt empty and sat by myself. The camp was quieting down, but I heard all sorts of conversations.

"Not here, Robert," Nancy whispered.

"Come on," Robert whispered back.

I looked around, trying to see them, but figured they were in the tall grass nearby. I was embarrassed to have heard them.

"This is not what I expected," I heard my mother say.

"Dreadful," my father said. "We cannot even be alone together."

I cupped my hands over my ears. Every conversation traveled through the plywood. I didn't want to hear any of it.

"What's wrong, Margaret?" Timmy asked.

I grabbed his hand and sprinted to the far gate of the camp. I pelted rocks over the fence until I was exhausted.

"Feel better?" Timmy asked.

"Not really," I said.

"Are you in love with John?"

"None of your beeswax."

"You going to dump me like Robert did?"

I clutched Timmy. "I'll never desert you. I love John, but that doesn't change things between us."

"Really?" Timmy looked ready to cry.

"Can I tell you a secret?"

Timmy nodded.

"John loves you, too."

Timmy hugged me back and sobbed. "I don't have anybody. Robert's got Nancy. You've got John. Mother and Father have each other."

"I need somebody," I said. "Would you be my buddy?"

"Legit?"

I nodded. "And when John comes for visits, he'll need to see you, too."

We didn't get back to the stall until Robert was back from Nancy's. Timmy and I exchanged knowing glances and lay down.

Within a week, Timmy had dysentery, like many people in the camp. He spent several days in the doctor's quarters. The poor sanitary conditions made it worse. The older Issei were susceptible to disease, as were the very young. I walked by the doctor's quarters and noticed an old woman lying on the floor. When I went in, I realized she was dead. I bent over in the weeds, heaving until my head stopped whirling. That was the first dead person I had ever seen. We had had pets die, but never a person. She was left lying there for most of the day.

"John, I feel like I've done something wrong," I said the next day.

"You haven't."

"Then why are we treated like we did?"

"Because the government is run by a bunch of hysterical drips."

John and his mother came every day as April stretched into May. John's parents allowed him to take a week off school to help us get settled. He and Mrs. Wilson brought food and other extras for us. I was terrified the guards would stop allowing them in. What would I do?

"What about school?" I asked John.

"Next week I'll have to get back to classes, but I'll be here on the weekends. I hate the idea of not seeing you every day."

"Me too."

My father helped other families plant gardens. They made the camp as homey as possible. And planting involved lots of work and lots of time.

Sports became an obsession for the kids who had nothing to do. Like Timmy.

"I'll be like John," Timmy said. "I'll play basketball and football and baseball."

"I'll help you with baseball," Robert said.

"Don't bother," Timmy snapped.

Because it was almost the end of the school year, most kids weren't forced to attend any more classes for that semester. Many parents figured they'd be back home by the start of another school year.

The second Saturday of May, I was surprised to see Elizabeth Parks walk toward our stall.

"Elizabeth!" I cried.

"Margaret, there you are," she said, relieved. "I was afraid I wasn't going to find you." We hugged each other. She looked around and said, "I can't believe they're doing this to you."

"What are you doing here?" I asked.

"I've missed you at school." She put her head down. "I feel just terrible about what's happening to your family."

"It's not your fault," I said.

"I brought you something." She held out a basket. I lifted the lid and saw fruits and cheese and crackers.

"This looks divine."

"I just wish I could do more."

"Did you drive out here yourself?"

Elizabeth nodded. "My parents forbade me to, but I had to see you."

That day, my family dined on the basket of food that Elizabeth brought. It was *heavenly*, compared to the food served in the mess halls. I went to sleep that night grateful for my friend, feeling almost happy once again.

On the last Saturday of May, John came without his parents.

"We've got a whole day together," he said. "I brought us a picnic."

John usually brought us fresh fruit. To get inside the fairgrounds, he had to give up some of it to the guards, but it was worth it.

"It can be like we're out on a date again," John said, clutching my hand.

We strolled all through the fairgrounds, and every time we saw a small nook, we surprised some other couple or small group of people. We finally went to a corner where some old equipment was stored. There was an abandoned tractor, just right for two people to hide behind.

John and I crawled behind the tractor, wrapping our arms around each other.

"Since that first night in the fairgrounds, the only time I've allowed myself to cry was with you," I said.

"I love you." John stroked my hair. Most of that day, we sat together, talking softly, and kissing each other.

"When is graduation?" I asked.

"June fifth. I'm not going."

"Why not?"

"It's a Saturday. I'd rather spend that time with you."

"But it's your graduation."

"It's supposed to be Robert's too."

After a couple of undisturbed hours, we peeled off our clothes and made love, clinging to each other. "There aren't words for what I'm feeling," I said.

We dozed. Why did war have to complicate the beauty?

When we strolled back to our stall in the evening, I knew something was wrong.

"Where's Mother?" I asked.

"Barbara is having the baby," Father answered.

John and I ran as fast as possible to the doctor's quarters—a few stalls in the largest barn. The doctors were still setting up beds and getting everything as sterile as possible. It looked absolutely primitive to me.

"How is she?"

"The baby is breech," Mother said.

CHAPTER 18
Audrey

My heart froze. "Can I see her?" I crept into the stall and saw my sister lying on a cot. Her face was drenched with sweat. I stroked her hair. "Can I do anything?"

She grimaced. "Not unless you can get this baby out of me."

I felt the tears coming.

"I'll be okay, Margaret. I figured I'd be in a hospital."

"Can't they take you to one?"

"The guards said the facilities were sufficient for having babies," Howard said. He looked scared.

"Everyone must leave now," the doctor said. "I'm going to turn the baby."

"Can Margaret stay with me?" Barbara asked, her eyes full of terror.

The doctor looked at me and nodded. I clutched Barbara's hand and prayed.

"There isn't much I can do for your pain," the doctor apologized. "We just don't have any medication yet."

Barbara grunted.

He started to turn the baby, pushing on the outside of Barbara's stomach and putting his hand inside to guide the

105

baby. I swallowed hard, not believing what I was seeing. Barbara clenched my hand harder. After what seemed like an eternity, the doctor smiled. "The baby cooperated. Now it should come out easier."

Barbara nodded. "I'm so tired."

"It's time to push," the doctor said.

Howard and I clasped our hands together behind her back to keep her up. After an hour, she lay back. "I can't do any more."

"Let's meet this new person," the doctor said. "The head is right here."

After a hard push and loud groan, I saw a head slide out.

"Stop," the doctor said. He cleaned the baby's nose out. "One more big push."

Barbara pushed again and out slipped her baby.

"It's a girl," the doctor said. Howard held the baby as the doctor tied off the cord, then wrapped up my niece. "She's a fighter."

Barbara smiled tiredly. "Can I hold her?"

"Just as soon as we deliver the placenta. You'll feel some tugging, but it shouldn't be as difficult as what you just did."

Soon Barbara held her daughter, with Howard's assistance. The doctor looked concerned. I scrambled around to where he sat and saw blood pouring from my sister.

"I need you to push right here," the doctor said, directing my hand into my sister's lower stomach.

"Is something wrong?" Howard asked.

"We need to stop the bleeding before I can stitch her up," the doctor explained.

I massaged my sister's stomach, but the blood wouldn't stop.

Barbara kissed her daughter's head. "You'd better take her now." She handed the baby to Howard and closed her eyes.

"Doctor!" I cried.

"I don't have any way of stopping the bleeding."

Howard rushed out of the room with the baby and came back with my parents. Father held the baby as Mother held Barbara. She stroked Barbara's hair and whispered to her.

"Barbara, please, wake up!" Howard yelled. He sounded hysterical.

I grabbed Barbara's hand and squeezed, but there was no response. I checked her pulse, and there was none. "I'm sorry, Barbara." I leaned over and kissed her cheek. "I love you." I cradled her head for a few minutes, feeling like I would explode. "Futz!" I screamed and kicked the floor.

Howard sobbed and rocked with her still body. He and Barbara had been sweethearts since senior year of high school. "I can't live without you," he chanted.

The doctor wiped his own tears away. "I'm so sorry."

I took the baby from my father's arms. As I held my new niece, I felt trapped between instant love and instant grief. "Hello there, sunshine." I kissed her gently and thought my heart would break. Barbara gladly gave her life for her baby. Would I ever be so unselfish?

A growing bitterness seeped out of me as our situation grew more cruel. The next day, we approached the center officials to make arrangements for Barbara. Mr. and Mrs. Wilson came with us.

"You can't bury the body in the fairgrounds," the center's director explained.

"May we take her and bury her then?" I asked.

"You cannot leave."

"Can we make arrangements for Barbara?" Mr. Wilson asked.

"The body will be buried in a local cemetery."

"Why can't Mr. and Mrs. Wilson take care of this?" I cried. "They're like family."

The director sneered at me. "Yes, I know that."

"Let me get this straight," Mr. Wilson said. "Because we're friends with the Yamaguchis, you won't let us make funeral arrangements for their daughter, who died as a result of being in this assembly center?"

The director looked from John to me. "I'm not willing to bend the rules this time."

"I can't believe he's being so cruel." I wiped an angry tear from my cheek as we left the director's office. "We can't even say our goodbyes properly."

Mr. Wilson put his hand on my father's shoulder. "I'll track down where they take Barbara. We'll visit and take flowers. I know that can't replace her family, but . . ."

Father smiled sadly. "You are a good man. Good friend."

As May ended, we celebrated the life of a new baby in our family.

"Barbara wanted to name her Audrey," Howard said.

"It's a beautiful name." I cuddled the baby.

We mourned the loss of my beautiful sister with a private, simple goodbye service. If she had been taken to the hospital to have her baby, she would probably have lived. Instead, she died in a stall, like some animal. I now knew how death felt.

CHAPTER 19
Midway

By June 2, no Japanese, citizen or alien, were allowed on the West Coast. On June 3, everyone in the "assembly center" heard the news of the Battle of Midway.

"Japan's fleet is crippled," Father said.

"That should end any chance of a Japanese invasion of America," I said.

"Now our country's leaders will see that we are no threat," Father said. "This should be the end of our time here."

"I hope so," I said, relieved that my father was smiling.

That afternoon, on John's daily visit, I shared my enthusiasm. He hugged me tight. "It will be nice to get you alone again. I miss smooching with you."

We waited with anticipation for our release to begin. I waited the following day, through the weekend, actually hoping we'd be out in time for graduation ceremonies. But we remained.

Everyone in our family doted on Audrey. Mother and Father held her, rocked her, and cooed to her. I had never seen them so entranced. Timmy played and talked with her constantly. He was so gentle and so attentive. It seemed like he was releasing his emotions by playing with his niece.

On June 7, DeWitt completed the removal of 100,000 Japanese Americans from Military Areas 1 and 2. Those areas were essentially free of Japanese. Rather than allowing us home, it seemed hatred was more pronounced than ever.

"I don't understand," I said. "I thought we'd be free to go home after Japan lost the Battle of Midway."

"This is not right." Father's voice shook.

"Japan can't harm America, so why are we still kept as prisoners?"

As the days crept by with no news of impending release, everyone resigned themselves to longer stays.

"We do not have a choice, do we?" Mother said as she weeded her flowers.

Communities sprouted within the fairgrounds, like my mother's flowers. Doctors, ministers, gardeners, and teachers used their abilities and talents to make everyone's stay in the fairgrounds bearable. While we waited for transport to permanent relocation centers, we lived one day at a time.

On Flag Day, the young children performed a pageant for the adults. We sang "America the Beautiful" and said the Pledge of Allegiance before several skits of American history. Each child chose an event in our country's history, then combined those events into a play. We had Abraham Lincoln, George Washington, and several patriots. Timmy was Benjamin Franklin, flying his kites. It was something constructive to occupy everyone's time. And a way to show our patriotism, even in confinement.

I filled my diary with thoughts and feelings every morning. Then I filled my notebooks with essays and political happenings.

No one wants to discuss politics with me. Mother's only interested in the top layer of current events. Nancy doesn't care about politics. Robert's too busy with Nancy. Father has folded in on himself and doesn't speak much anymore. Writing allows me to cope with the changes in my life. I can get my thoughts on paper.

I'm watching Timmy continue to change. He seems less innocent than he did just a month ago. It's sad to think he's being tainted so deeply. I'm angry with Robert for deserting his little brother. I understand his wanting to be with Nancy, but our family needs him too. He's doing nothing to help us!

At least Timmy and I are spending time together. His beliefs are being tested, which is hard for a boy. His big brother is too busy for him. John can't be here. What else can I do for my little brother? He's drifting further away every day. I'm changing too. I'm angry with everyone. But I'm stronger.

June 17, Milton Eisenhower resigned as WRA director, because he disagreed with how the Japanese Americans were being uprooted.

I feel most deeply that when the war is over . . . we as Americans are going to regret the avoidable injustices that may have been done.

When I read about his resignation, I felt deserted. I had always felt he fought for us. I had heard he was disgusted by the quality of living forced upon us.

Dear Diary,

Who's on our side, now? With Eisenhower gone, who's to say what his replacement will do. There are so many hysterical politicians scared of people like me! Like my parents! What in the world could we do to the country?

The next day, Elizabeth arrived in camp again. "Until we moved to California, I had never seen a Japanese person."

"The majority of the Japanese are located on the West Coast," I said. "Or were."

"I don't understand such blanket hatred. You're no more the enemy than I am." Elizabeth handed me a basket.

I looked inside and saw fresh fruit and vegetables, bread, real butter, and strawberry jam. My eyes filled with tears. "This means the world to me."

On June 21, John visited again, looking devastated.

"What's wrong?" I asked.

"A huge SNAFU."

"You've been drafted."

"I leave next week."

I sucked in my breath. "How will I find you? How will you find me?" I panicked. John was my only remaining link to the outside world—to the real me. I thought my heart would burst out of my chest. "This was supposed to be a short-term stay, and we've been here almost two months already." My breath hitched as I talked. I fought dizziness, afraid I'd faint.

"I'll write to your Uncle Toshio as soon as I know my APO address. I'll have him forward it to you."

"What's an APO address?"

"Army Post Office."

My heart calmed a bit. John planted a kiss on me.

"The guards are staring," I whispered, my heart pounding.

"I don't care," John said into my ear.

"What if they don't let you in next time?" I closed my eyes. John stared at the guards. "They won't keep me from you."

Dear Diary,

The Battle of Midway seems to be going on inside of me. I am a prisoner because of my heritage, my ancestry. Something I had nothing to do with. John's leaving to fight in a war that's stupid and futile. I want to stop it, but how? Do I have any power? I feel outnumbered and out-maneuvered. My whole life is walking away from me. I only have a week to memorize every inch of him.

CHAPTER 20
Camp

John's goodbye was one of the hardest moments of my life.

Robert hugged John and said, "See you when you get back."

Timmy clung to John's waist and sobbed. "You can't go. You just can't."

John pried him off and gave him a big bear hug. "Take care of my baby while I'm away, okay?"

"How can I live without you?" I asked.

John smiled sadly. "You won't be without me. My heart's staying here."

"I don't know if I'm strong enough to do this."

"You have to be, my pearl. We have to be strong for each other."

Our last kiss seemed to linger forever, then it was gone too quickly. I stood alone at the gate, watching John's tail lights get smaller. Silent, angry tears slid down my face. This wasn't how my life was supposed to be.

On June 30, we were told we were leaving. "Finally," I said.

"I have heard the relocation centers are much nicer than this," Father agreed.

Audrey was the only one whose life wasn't disrupted. All she knew was she was loved. Mother was constantly sewing baby clothes. Audrey smiled and giggled at us and helped me see beauty. She made John's being drafted a bit easier for me.

We piled into buses, but weren't told our destination. I pulled out my notebook.

As families board, I see proud, angry faces. The ride itself is quiet. A resentful resignation seems to permeate through the bus. Instead of returning to our real lives, we are being carted somewhere like livestock. We are not allowed to have the window shades open, so the bus is dark. I'm writing this as we bump along, not knowing what lies ahead for me or for my family. How long will we live under prison conditions? Will the camp be better than the assembly center? Could it be any worse?

We transferred onto trains. We were not allowed to raise shades or leave our seats except to go to the bathroom. Every time we stopped, I hoped we had found our destination, but each time it was a false alarm. At one stop, we were allowed to lift the shades, and to my surprise, I saw Japanese people walking around the train station.

"This is pathetic," I said. "If we had left with Uncle Toshio, we could still be walking around wherever we wanted."

"Instead we can't even leave our seats without permission," Robert said.

At the last train stop, we were once again loaded onto buses and shipped further. We finally arrived at our new home, the relocation camp, as the government called it. As I got off the bus, my eyes adjusted to a flat, desolate landscape. The sign on the gate said "Colorado River Relocation Center, Poston, Arizona."

"Arizona?" I asked. "They're putting us in the desert." At first, my legs wouldn't move. I sat down on my suitcase. All I saw were army barracks. There weren't any houses or cottages, as we were led to believe. The government could call it whatever they wanted, but it was an internment camp.

Soldiers marched us to a mess hall, where they recorded our numbers. Everyone had to fill out forms, supply fingerprints, and take physical exams. We stripped down in front of several other people, stood around, and waited. I held my head high and refused to give in to the humiliation.

Guards searched us. They seized anything considered dangerous, like kitchen knives. They emptied an old Issei woman's purse and snatched her knitting needles.

A woman screamed, "That's for my baby's milk. You can't take it!"

The guards took away the woman's hot plate. They issued each of us a cot, a blanket, and a sack for our mattress, just like at the fairgrounds.

After the embarrassment of the registration process, we finally found out our address. It was block 12, row 6, unit C. We plodded and trudged through the huge camp until we finally found block 12.

I found row 6, and discovered unit C in the middle. I pushed open the door and could have fallen over. "This is it?" I asked. "For five people?" The room was about 25 by 20 feet, the largest size apartment.

"Our kitchen at home was bigger than this," Timmy said.

Each block of apartments had twelve rows of barracks. In the center of each block stood a mess hall, plus a laundry room and the showers and toilets.

"I really need to use one," I said.

"I will escort you," Mother said.

As we entered the bathroom, I realized the toilets didn't have stalls. There was a concrete slab down the center of the room, where toilet bowls were arranged in pairs, back to back.

"There's no privacy!" I cried. "We could hold hands sitting on the toilet."

"We are being treated without dignity," Mother agreed. "I will stand in front of you, then you do the same for me."

When Mother and I returned from the bathroom, we entered our new home and realized it was almost as bad as the fairgrounds. One bare light bulb dangled from the ceiling. No furniture. Nothing. The barracks were built with quarter-inch boards over a wooden frame and covered with tar paper. I knew instantly I would have no more privacy in this place than I had in the fairgrounds. I vowed to find a way to get through this. If I didn't, I would completely disappear.

Nancy knocked on our door. "We're over two rows."

I felt like crying. I missed my old room now more than ever. I missed being able to close the bathroom door and take long bubble baths. I missed gabbing on the phone with John. Mostly, I missed John. I felt so empty, I wanted to give up.

I noticed my father gathering scrap lumber, as he had done in the fairgrounds. I joined him, and tried to be positive, though my heart felt fractured.

As I sat in the mess hall during supper, I realized what I could do to help. How I could make use of my time—a newspaper. A camp paper. I had been looking for some outlet for my writing and a way to stop mooning over John. I didn't know how long we'd be prisoners in the camp, but it would fill up my days and help me funnel my angry energy into something constructive.

CHAPTER 21
Adjustments

Like at the fairgrounds, I noticed guards in their towers, pointing their guns at us. Rather than be intimidated, I was filled with rage. I glared at them every time I was near the towers.

Father and Robert built some shelves and a table. They measured and nailed boards together, using discarded, crooked nails and the heels of their shoes.

Mother piled our clothes onto a "bed." I dug through the meager mound and pulled out a pair of jeans and a blouse. "My dresses and skirts are getting filthy."

"More sensible," Mother approved.

Robert and Father built a skinny, rectangular box and pounded nails onto the back wall. "A closet," Father said proudly.

"What's this material from?" I asked as Mother and I made curtains.

"Bed sheets. Since we will not need them, we might as well use them."

As the men hammered, we stitched and laughed. When we were finished, the curtains allowed us each a small amount of personal space. I felt better already. I was grateful for Mother's resourcefulness.

"There's enough scrap lumber here to build a small porch," Robert said.

"It would add to the amount of room we have," Father agreed. "We are fortunate to have found so much."

Timmy raced from Robert to Father. "Can I help?" he asked.

Father managed to pipe water in from an outside faucet and Robert pieced together a small kitchen. He crafted a sink and cupboards out of scrap material. Timmy collected tin can lids, and we nailed them over holes in the walls.

Mother clasped her hands. "If we have this much love, we will be just fine."

I felt so alone those first few days. I was restless and impatient with everyone.

"Margaret?" Mother asked.

"I thought having Robert and Nancy around would make this easier, but it makes it harder."

"Because they are together?"

"I'm glad they're together, but they're *always* together. I can't talk to one without the other."

"It is hard when your friend falls in love."

"I feel so alone. Every time they kiss or touch, it reminds me that . . ." I paused, feeling suddenly self-conscious about talking with my mother.

"That John is not here?"

"I miss him, Mother. What if he dies?"

"You must have faith that he will not. Tell me about your writing."

My mother had never asked me about my writing before. She was proud of everything I did—I knew that, but she normally didn't ask questions. She left questions for Father.

I gave her some of my essays to read and held my breath.

"These are quite good," Mother said. "They sound professional."

"This is what I want to do, Mother. I want to write."

"Then you should."

That evening, I shut myself away behind a curtain, creating my privacy.

Dear Diary,

I miss Barbara terribly. Every time I see Audrey, I see Barbara's eyes. How I love that little girl. She simply shines. Barbara would have made a wonderful mother. She must be watching us from heaven, our guardian angel. I think maybe she gave us Audrey as a reminder of the beauty hidden in this ugly time. Whenever I'm feeling blue, I pick up Audrey and she gives me a lift. What a gift!

I wrote to my cousin Dorothy. She sent me a letter back right away. In it, she told me about their home in Denver and the large Japanese population. The more I read of her letter, the more I ached to be out of the camp. I was still angry with my father. Life wasn't easy for Uncle Toshio and his family—money was scarce, and he could find only temporary jobs. But they were free. They didn't live behind barbed wire and gun barrels. Dorothy had met a boy, and they were going steady. Big surprise! She could touch and kiss her beau. I didn't know if mine was alive.

Margaret, I realize how much of a bug-eyed Betty I was when you and John started dating. I was so jealous. As you know, I was slack happy over him. I must have looked like such a bimbo, trying to steal him from you. I'm sorry. I'm glad I didn't succeed. You two love each other.

I'll find that someday. I love you.

Dot

I wandered to Nancy's room, but Robert was over there.

"Hi, Margaret," Nancy said.

"Can we talk?"

We hooked arms and started strutting, like we used to do at home.

"I'm so lonely," I said. "I just feel like screaming."

"I know, lamb pie. When Robert leaves at night to go home, I want to just cry. I practically run across camp in the morning to meet him."

I hinged a glance at Nancy from the corner of my eye. Did she really think our situations were the same? Her guy was here, every day. Mine got shot at, every day. I knew she wouldn't understand and decided to end the conversation. It made me sadder. And more resentful. Instead, we strolled the camp silently. Through the silence, I discovered I didn't want to be with Nancy as much as I thought I did. I didn't need her like I once had. I was changing, growing. Was I outgrowing our friendship?

As the days went on, my talks with my mother became more regular. She was genuinely interested in my paper idea, and it helped to bounce ideas off her. My depression lifted. I realized I was forming a friendship with my mom.

CHAPTER 22
A Different Life

People fabricated lives for themselves in the camp. Scrap lumber was gathered and used, seeds were planted, friends were found. Slowly, sports teams formed. Doctors and nurses tended to patients; teachers prepared for the following year, hoping they would be home by then; and housewives ordered their barracks as best they could. Both churches and temples sprouted in the camp, though I wondered if God really existed.

One afternoon, I walked around the camp, noticing the make-up of the people. I figured about half the population were women and a quarter were school-aged children. How long could we live like this? Our camp was located in a desolate part of Arizona. When the sun was high, the temperature was in the hundreds. Many times, movement within the camp stopped when the heat became unbearable. When the wind blew, dirt whirled everywhere, even with the doors closed.

As I hiked through the camp, I was shocked to see non-Japanese. "Excuse me," I asked one Caucasian man, "are you visiting?"

"I'm here with my wife and children." He smiled at me.

"You willingly came to live in the camp?"

"What else could I do? I love my family."

That man restored some of my faith in my fellow Americans. Not everyone thought we deserved to be in the camps.

I watched a very pregnant woman, not much older than me, struggle to carry a box. I thought of Barbara.

"Can I help you?" I ran over to her.

"Thank you," she said. "I'm such a whale, I can't do anything."

"Where's your husband?" I noticed her wedding band.

"He's serving in the war."

"And they still put you in here?"

She nodded bitterly. "As far as the government is concerned, a drop of Japanese blood taints a person."

I wrote constantly—about the injustices I saw, about the irony of some of the situations. I wrote John every day. I felt like a part of me had been ripped away. But I could almost reconnect that part in my letters to him.

As I was folding a letter to John, Timmy said, "Stick this in the envelope."

"What is it?"

"Just a note to John. I've been practicing my jump shot, like he showed me."

After the first couple of weeks in camp, we settled into our routines. Robert and Nancy spent all their time together, so I didn't see much of either of them.

I felt isolated. "Isn't there anything to do?" I asked my mother.

"There is not much to help with, daughter. We do not cook our meals. Our room does not require much cleaning." She touched my face with her hand. "Go visit Howard and your niece."

I wandered to Howard's room. "Want some company?"

Howard was lying on his bed, holding Audrey. "You're always welcome, Mar."

"Audrey's getting so big, Howard. Want me to take her for a while?"

"I'll catch a nap if you do."

Howard rolled toward the wall. All he wanted to do any-more was sleep. I scooped up Audrey and took her for an outing. I loved every moment I spent with her. I felt Barbara's presence whenever I watched my niece. Audrey calmed me.

"Mar, wait up!" Timmy called.

We took turns carrying Audrey back to our room. Timmy came alive when he was with Audrey. He talked softly and sweetly to her, and made faces at her. He loved the attention as much as she did. I enjoyed watching the two of them. The affection was so apparent in Timmy's eyes. Connecting with Timmy and Audrey helped me feel useful and youthful.

My father immersed himself in plants and tended to a com-munity garden along one side of our barracks. Anyone who wanted to help was welcome and was promised some of the vegetables when they were ready.

Dear Diary,

I've been watching my father without his knowing it. He looks happy. The garden supplies his purpose in the camp. Some of the men don't have a purpose. They choose to sit in their rooms. Many look sad and angry. Because they no longer provide for their families, they're giving up. I'm proud of my father for making the best of this awful situation, even though he seems more fragile now. He could make any-thing grow anywhere. I have no talent with green things, so I'll make sketches of him in my journal.

In late July, Robert and Nancy came to our barracks with Nancy's parents.

"We have news," Nancy said. She looked prettier than I ever remembered.

"We're going to be married," Robert gushed.

"That's super!" I hugged them, noticing four shocked faces.

"You are so young," Mother said truthfully.

Robert took Mother's hands and kissed her forehead. "We love each other."

"This is a good thing," Father said. He hugged Robert, then Nancy. "You are a daughter already."

"When?" Mrs. Sato asked.

"Next week!" Nancy said.

Timmy jumped up and ran off. I started to follow, but Father put his hand on my shoulder. He shook his head.

"I didn't mean to . . . ," Robert said.

"He is having difficulty accepting your leaving the family," Mother said.

"But I'm not leaving."

"You already have, my son." Mother smiled and kissed Robert's cheek.

"How will we make Nancy's dress?" Mrs. Sato asked Mother.

"She would look lovely in a simple A-line dress, would she not?"

"I wonder if the children will end up living nearby," Father said to Mr. Sato.

"They will be a brand-new family and need their own apartment."

I walked away from the barracks with Robert and Nancy.

"Holy Joe," I said. "I can't believe you're getting married."

"Life's so different in here," Nancy said. "There's really no reason to wait."

I felt even more distant now. Soon, I would have no one left. They wouldn't mean to abandon me, but they would. Once they were married, they had to start different lives. That meant I had to find a different life for myself.

"Would you stand up for us?" Robert asked.

"I'd be honored," I said.

"If we'd known this a month ago, we could have asked John," Nancy said.

"I'm so afraid for him," I said.

Robert put his hand on my shoulder. "He'll come back to you."

"How can you know that?"

"He'll do whatever it takes."

The following Wednesday evening, Robert and Nancy married in the makeshift church, with Father and me as witnesses and the rest of our families watching. Many people attended, though we didn't know everyone. It was an event, a reason to feel happy. I watched as Howard sat beside Mother and held Audrey on his lap.

Since Barbara's death, he had fallen apart. Mother helped with Audrey, and we tried to include him in our family. But he looked terrible. He started weeping at the ceremony and bolted, leaving Audrey with us. As soon as the wedding was over, I chased after him and found him in his barracks, holding one of Barbara's blouses. I put my hand on his shoulder and sat down beside him.

"I can't go on without her," he said. "I can't do it, Margaret."

"You have to. For your daughter."

"Barbara was so beautiful. And smart. She was so special."

"I miss her too."

"I know Audrey will always have a home with your family," Howard said.

"Applesauce! You have to go on with life, for Audrey." I left my brother-in-law sleeping that evening. I thought about my newborn niece. She had a rough start in life, but proved she was a fighter. I just hoped her father would choose to stick around and see her grow up. I returned to our barracks, in time for wedding cake. Someone in the kitchen managed to bake a small white cake.

"I wish it could have been fancier," Nancy admitted.

"It doesn't matter," I said. "The cake is secondary."

Robert and Nancy left as husband and wife to their own apartment. The camp director housed them two blocks away from us, so they had to trek a long way. I rocked Audrey to sleep as tears of jealousy and guilt streamed down my cheeks.

CHAPTER 23
Letters

July 28, 1942
Dear Margaret,

I miss seeing you every day like we used to. I'm so sorry your family is stuck in that loathsome camp. My father still feels responsible. Like he should have stayed with your family. I just wish you would have come with us. My father misses your father and all of you. He's trying to get your family out of the camp and here with us. Please write when you can. You're in my thoughts.

Dot

Growing up, Dorothy and I had been close, not just as cousins, but as friends. She lived across town. We saw each other at school, but as we got older, we found our interests didn't match. She was a cheerleader at school and enjoyed home economics. I was on the paper and taking advanced classes. She was a social butterfly, with boyfriends too numerous to mention. I was more reserved; my only boyfriend was John. And yet, I adored her. Our only big tiff had been over John.

The next day I opened another letter with Uncle Toshio's address. John! I ran to a shady spot near our barracks, and ripped open the envelope.

Dear Margaret,

I miss you so much, beautiful. At your request, I won't mention any scuttlebutt. It's never uplifting. I hope your family is well. I wish Nancy and Robert's being together didn't make you feel so sad and alone, although if I was in your situation, I'd probably feel the same way. Try to meet a deb. Just don't find someone to replace me!

There are a bunch of croots in my company who've gotten Dear John letters from their sweethearts. They go out chasing skirts every chance they get. They try to get me to go, but I'm not interested. After loving you, no one else could compare. You're it! My baby!!!

I guess all my letters are Dear John, aren't they? I just hope none will ever mean you don't love me anymore. I don't know when I'll get a chance to write again, so don't worry about me, okay? I'm on maneuvers. I've got my pea shooter. As soon as I can, I'll return to you. Love me, but don't worry about me. Find something constructive to occupy your time. I know you'll make a difference there, just as you did on the Sentinel and in my life. Life has to go on, and you're strong enough to get through anything. Pray for this to end.

I love you,
John

By the end of the letter, I was sobbing. I reread it several times. Touching the paper was like connecting to John. His fingers had held the paper and folded it. I ran my fingers over the folds, imagining John's gentle hands when they slipped the letter in its envelope. It smelled faintly of John. It brought back all the memories of our first time together, the farm house, the moonlight. It was time to stop mooning and make a difference, like John suggested.

The next day, I stood up during breakfast in the mess hall. "If anyone wants to learn how to swing dance, I'll give lessons." When I sat down, my hands were shaking. By supper, I was glad I had my records and player.

Timmy and I tacked up posters, announcing a dance for that Saturday night.

"A dance?" a deb asked. "Here?"

"Might as well."

She looked at me kind of funny, then said, "Sounds smooth to me."

We transformed the mess hall into a huge dance floor. Although we had permission to have the dance, all the work was ours to do. Robert and Nancy helped Timmy and me move tables and chairs out of the way. Most of the camp showed up.

"Can I play the records?" Timmy asked.

"Don't scratch any."

Timmy spun swinging music, including Glenn Miller and all the big bands.

"This is too perfect!" cried Nancy. She and Robert danced to every song, like a school dance.

Howard wandered in.

"You have to cut a rug with me," I said, dragging him to the dance floor.

"I can't—Audrey," Howard protested.

I handed Audrey to Mother. We danced a mild version of the Lindy Hop.

"That was fun." Howard laughed. "Want to try another?" Lauren Richardsen, a professional singer, called the Lambeth Walk.

"Why, Howard, you're a regular cloud walker," I said.

"Barbara made me learn."

A slow dance began, and I held Howard. His body was stiff at first, but then he relaxed and held me too. We were like two lost bodies. There was no romance between us, just the comfort of someone's touch.

"Thanks, Mar," Howard said. "I needed to get out of my room for a while."

"We should do this every week," one woman said as she left.

A letter from Elizabeth was in my next bundle of mail.

August 5, 1942
Dear Margaret,

I just wanted you to know I've been thinking about you. School will be starting in another month. Will you be back? If I can do anything for you, please let me know.

Your friend,
Liz

I stuck the letter back into the envelope and thought about it.

Dear Diary,

Will I be back for the start of school? Unlikely. I'm trapped. I'm happy Elizabeth still wants to be my friend, but she's so far away. So removed from my life. I have trouble thinking of life outside the camp. It's time to forget the outside and do something on the inside.

The next day, I started my other idea: a camp newspaper.

"Do you have any suggestions for my newspaper, Father?" I asked at breakfast.

"Most people get local papers delivered," Father said. "Perhaps you should stick to the dancing lessons."

"But I can do more," I said. I looked at my mother. "My idea for a camp paper is to supplement the dry war news and offer something fun."

"It's a great idea," Robert said as he slid next to me. "Our local papers are just news about the lives we used to have. I think you could do a unique paper, mixing international news, camp politics, and some highlights of the week."

"A weekly paper?"

"I'll help you if you want."

"I'd like that." I glanced around. "Where's Nancy?"

"She wasn't feeling well this morning." Robert looked down at his breakfast. "I let her get some extra sleep."

"Is she okay?" I asked. "Is it something serious or just a flu?"

"Something like the flu," Robert said.

CHAPTER 24
Camouflage

I made my way across the camp to Nancy's apartment and knocked on the door.

"Come in," Nancy said softly.

I tiptoed into a darkened room. Nancy lay on her cot. "Are you okay?" I asked, sitting on the floor beside her, afraid to touch her.

"I can't move without heaving."

"I brought you some tea." I placed the mug on the floor. I caressed Nancy's hand. "Remember when we both had the flu at the same time?"

"Our folks and all our teachers thought we were faking it to get out of classes."

"Do you need the doctor?" I asked, my throat tight.

Nancy shook her head. "I just can't seem to sleep enough lately."

I sat in the room, holding Nancy's hand, until she snored. I stroked her hair away from her face and kissed her forehead. She looked very fragile on that cot, and my chest hitched. I quietly left her as she snoozed, praying all the way home.

I spent the rest of the day playing peekaboo and pat-a-cake with Audrey. I forgot about where I was and what I didn't have. When I played with that little girl, I entered into her world of innocence. If only the innocence could last.

"There are no Japanese in California or any of the other military areas in the western states that were evacuated," I said, reading an article from the August 7 *Valle Verde Gazette*.

"They evacuated every Japanese?" Father asked.

"Over one hundred thousand Japanese have been removed and interned." I stared at him.

"How many camps are there?"

"Ten camps. Poston has about eighteen thousand people." Father's eyes widened. "So many?"

I swallowed hard. "I wonder if the rest of the country knows what's happening in California and in the camps."

"The country must know." Father's voice was soft and tentative.

"Elizabeth told me she had never even seen a Japanese person until moving to California. It makes me question if the country is really behind the decision to imprison us, or if citizens even know where we were sent."

Robert helped me organize the inaugural issue of the camp paper.

"I think the first one should include international news blurbs, camp highlights, like births, deaths, and marriages, and an editorial," I said.

"You should do one on the internment. Let everyone see who you are."

"Me?"

"You're the editor of this camp paper."

"That wasn't what I had in mind."

"Like it or not, Mar, this is your baby. It's your chance."

Robert was right, of course.

In this first issue of what I hope will become a regular camp paper, it's important we all know and realize the injustice of our situation. None of us in this camp are dangerous. Those who are dangerous aliens are behind prison walls somewhere. None of us deserve to be treated as criminals. One way to change our situation is to let our feelings be known. We cannot give up our former lives or our freedom without a fight. This is my fight.

I offer this paper as an alternative to the biased news we are receiving from our hometown newspapers.

"Can I help you?" Timmy asked.

"You could deliver them to various spots around camp," I said.

"As long as I don't have to be around Robert."

"Timmy! Why are you so mad at him?"

"He chose her over us."

"Nancy?" I put my arm around Timmy's shoulder. "He loves her. He didn't abandon us. He just got married."

Timmy shrugged. "Same thing." He delivered papers with a wagon.

After that issue, people came forward to help out.

"I was a reporter in my county," one man said.

"I draw political cartoons," a woman said at breakfast. "I have a great idea."

"And I write humor," another woman said.

I smiled. "Anyone who wants to work on it is welcome."

By the next week, we had someone to cover different aspects of camp: sports teams, schedule of events, camp life.

"You need a photographer?" an older man asked me one evening.

"That would be super," I said.

"I'll have to show the proofs to the camp administrator and get approval for the use of each picture."

"Sounds like you've done this before," I said.

"I sent some photos to my relatives that moved inward."

"This is so neat," I said, pleased that so many people wanted to help.

"You can focus on being the editor and delegate the grunt jobs," Robert said.

"What?" I asked.

"Let them scoop out the stories. You're best at editorials and political essays. Concentrate your efforts on those and let the other people do the running around."

I grinned. "Would you help me with the layout?"

Dear Diary,

My life has a routine. I teach dance steps and conduct weekly dances in the mess hall. People look forward to it. Between the dances and the paper, I'm very busy and hardly have time to think about Nancy. When I do, I feel almost guilty for not thinking about her more often. She isn't getting any sicker, but it worries me she isn't getting any better either.

I try to spend time with her, but feel myself drifting away. I enjoy activities in which Nancy has no interest.

I still wrote to John every day. Usually right after lunch I headed for my tree. It helped me organize my thoughts and gave me something to look forward to. I realized I was feeling happier than I had in a long time.

"I guess John was right, Mother," I said at supper. "I needed to focus my attention on *doing* something. I feel like I'm accomplishing things now."

"That is good. Everyone must have jobs and goals." Mother grabbed my hand. "I watch after Timmy and tend to my flowers."

As we left the mess hall one morning, I watched camp officials tack up posters.

"The Department of Labor issues an urgent request for agricultural workers for Montana, Colorado, Utah, Idaho," I read. "The Nisei are urged to prove their patriotism by saving the harvest in these four states. Only the Nisei, or American-born Japanese, are allowed to participate in the program." The Issei, or Japanese-born Japanese, couldn't participate since they were aliens. "It says the crops are about to rot because most of the men have reported for military duty."

"Or working in defense plants," Robert added.

"Are you going to apply?"

"Why should I? A few months ago, I was labeled the enemy." Robert balled his fist. "Now they want me to help save the harvest? Forget it."

Robert wasn't alone. Many Nisei had grown bitter at their situation and refused to help, which fueled my thoughts for another essay:

> *Many Nisei in our camp are resentful at the request they save the harvest for other Americans. The Nisei were American citizens by birth and still ended up in an internment camp. However, 10,000 Nisei from various camps jumped at a reprieve from the camp. They enrolled in the 60-day program. The only state to refuse Japanese workers was California, which hired 30,000 Mexican workers.*

By August 18, the War Department assigned the camps to making camouflage nets. This meant job opportunities for internees. The nasty work forced people to wear masks and gloves to protect their skin from chemicals on the netting.

"What an irony. They don't trust us to live on the coast as their neighbors, but they want us to make camouflage nets for their soldiers," Robert said. "And pick their crops while we eat rotting food. What piffle!"

I knew he was still angry he couldn't fight in the war, but I had hoped marrying Nancy had cooled him down some.

At the end of the month, Nancy and I had a rare moment alone. "Are you going to finish high school here?" I asked her.

Nancy shook her head. "We don't have to go now, since we're past sixteen."

"But I'm so bored. I'd like to get my diploma on schedule so I can go to college."

"I won't be going to college."

I sat silent. Nancy was different now. I didn't know how to respond to her. The wedge between us was growing, and I didn't know how to make it smaller.

"Lamb pie, we haven't told anybody yet, but I'm pregnant."

I grabbed Nancy's hand. "That's wonderful, doll." I stopped. "But how can you know that already? You've only been married a few weeks."

Nancy looked at me with her eyebrows raised. "We haven't been able to keep our hands off each other since we started dating . . ."

"Oh." I sometimes felt so naive. I never *suspected* Nancy might be pregnant. I felt even lonelier.

"We were going to get married anyhow. You don't think I'm a hot cake, do you?"

I laughed. "No, Nancy. You love each other. How far along are you?"

"Almost three months."

"I won't spill your secret," I said. "Even though I don't think it would matter."

"I know I haven't been around much lately, Margaret."

"I thought you didn't have time for me." I slipped John's ring on and off my thumb.

"I know," Nancy said. "Sorry." Nancy paused, then looked at me. "Margaret, did you and John, you know . . . play nookie?"

"Not at first. I waited until I was sure he wasn't just wolfing me."

"You truly thought John would drop you?"

"You heard the stories about him."

"But, he was dizzy over you, from the beginning."

"I know that now. But he was my first." I blushed. "I wish I had gotten pregnant."

"Why?"

"I'm just so afraid he won't come back."

"Margaret, you can't think like that."

"I can't help it. I made him promise me that he wouldn't tell me anything about the war in his letters—where he's at, what battles he's fighting, nothing. It's silly, but if we don't talk about his being part of it, somehow the war doesn't exist for us."

"That isn't silly. I'm so relieved that Robert can't fight. He still wants to."

"John went because he had to."

Nancy and I gossiped into the night, until Robert brought us supper. They went to their apartment, and I ambled. Having shot the breeze with Nancy so intimately made me feel better. We were connected again. I hoped they would tell the parents soon about the baby. But I was worried for Nancy. I remembered Barbara.

As September started, so did school for the camp children. Up to age sixteen, school was a requirement. After that, it was a decision for the student and parents to make. I returned to school, one of only a handful of high school kids to do so.

I made high grades and helped organize a school paper. It wasn't as elaborate as my old one, but it was fun to work on.

"Margaret," a classmate said, "Would you help us plan a year book?"

"Sure," I said.

"We don't have any experience, and you seem to know what you're doing."

"How do you know me?"

"You taught the dancing. My name is Sharon Ito."

I smiled at the quiet girl. I remembered her from the dancing lessons. "Are you an artist?" I asked, noticing her portfolio.

"Not really."

I studied the sketch. "This is me?"

"It was one of the first lessons."

"Impressive," I said. "I dabble in sketches, but I'm not very good."

"This isn't very good either. My parents say I'm foolish for trying to be an artist."

"You're very talented."

Dear Diary,

Having another deb in the school helps ease my pain at losing Nancy as a girlfriend. We still see each other and talk, but it's different. She's caught up in being a wife and impending motherhood. I want to graduate from high school and prepare myself for college—for life after this camp. I feel very torn. Should I be more loyal to Nancy? Or should I fend for myself? After all, she hasn't been loyal to me since John's been in the army. I still love Nancy like my sister, but she's changing. I guess I'm changing too. But I like the person I'm becoming. Nancy is turning into our mothers. I want more than that. I want to be strong. I want to be interesting. I want something in addition to my family to bring me joy.

By the end of September, Nancy and Robert had to tell the family. She was starting to show and suffering terrible morning sickness.

"Mother, Father," Nancy said. "Mr. and Mrs. Yamaguchi, we have something to tell you. I'm pregnant."

Mother clapped her hands, as did Nancy's mother.

"Good," Father said. "A new life. This is good."

"When?" Mother asked.

Nancy shot a look my way and bit her lip.

"March," Robert said calmly, holding Nancy's hand.

The smiles froze on the Satos' faces. "You will not have been married long enough."

"Is this why you chose to marry?" Father asked quietly.

"No," Robert said firmly. "We didn't mean for a baby to come this quickly. It just pushed our wedding ahead a little faster."

"Unacceptable," Mr. Sato shouted. "You did this to my daughter."

"I am disappointed," Father said. "I thought we had taught you properly."

Nancy started to cry. "I thought it wouldn't matter, since we're in this grim place." She put her hands over her face.

I stood up, my heart pounding. "Can I say something? Can't you see Robert and Nancy love each other?" I looked at all the parents, then stood by Nancy. "Does it really matter when this baby was conceived? Won't you four love this baby?"

"I will love it," Mother said. "But I disapprove."

"They're not asking you to approve or disapprove. If we hadn't ended up living like animals, this wouldn't have happened. And we wouldn't have lost Barbara."

Mrs. Sato sat up, took her daughter's hands, and then hugged her. "It does not matter. We love you, and we will love your baby."

"After all, it isn't like they're the first two humans to do this," I shrugged.

"That does not make it proper," Father said.

"There's joy waiting to come into our lives—a new baby."

The two soon-to-be grandfathers sat staring forward, not budging.

"I will consider your words," Father said, then he went into our apartment.

CHAPTER 25
Anything but Leave

Dear Diary,

Halloween. I'm adjusting to the school within the internment camp. Despite prison-like surroundings, I actually enjoy going to school each day. I help with the paper and the yearbook, and I'm meeting new kids who are becoming my friends. I don't feel quite as isolated as I did. I have a purpose every morning—a reason to get up and get dressed.

The only problem is the schoolwork itself. My classes are easy. I don't have the option of taking advanced courses here in the camp like I had in Valle Verde. Because I've already completed my English and math requirements for graduation, my work load is considerably smaller than it was in my high school. I'm not being challenged.

"Could I graduate at the end of this year?" I asked the teacher.

"What would you do?"

"College correspondence courses."

The days turned to weeks. My father struggled with his feelings about Nancy's pregnancy. He kept busy, but the baby was never far from his thoughts. He was distracted and became agitated whenever Robert came over.

Dorothy wrote to me, telling me about how they were settling into Denver. She attended school and wasn't experiencing the prejudice she had in California. Uncle Toshio had found a good job in a factory. I was happy to hear from my cousin, but it made me think about the job situation in the camp.

The government paid camp workers. Doctors, cooks, farmers, and teachers were able to earn money, but it was usually significantly less than what white workers received. And there weren't enough jobs to go around. Those who had no skills—who were either too old or too ill to work—many times felt useless in the camp. The elderly, especially, had nothing to do. They couldn't help their families cook or clean like they had before evacuation. I saw many older Japanese simply sit and wait to die.

In the Halloween issue of the camp paper I ran a story about the pay discrepancy and how some in the camp reacted.

Nisei doctors in our camp hospitals earn nineteen dollars a month. They perform the same work as white doctors, who earn their normal pay—more than fifty times as much as the Nisei. Many times, workers in the camp are not paid on time. A breakdown of the pay scale is as follows: unskilled workers receive twelve dollars a month and professionals receive nineteen dollars. A soldier in the U.S. Army receives twenty-one dollars a month.

Due to the blatant favoritism in wages, some men in the camp have started a co-op, where internees can purchase needed items and support one another. Several men have pooled money. That money has allowed others to start businesses, such as a general store. It is like a bank in camp, for those who participate. Businesses within the camp will make it feel like our own city.

Robert volunteered at the hospital, working about twenty hours a week.

"You're helping the doctors out a lot," I said.

"I'm gaining practical experience for medical school," Robert answered.

"You still want to be a doctor?"

"Might even be a surgeon."

With the cooler weather, my father had less gardening work to do. He had started walking the perimeter of the camp. One evening, my father looked troubled.

"What is it, Father?"

"I am sad this night."

"Why?"

"I no longer provide for my family." Father looked down.

"You grow the most wonderful food."

"I cannot sell it. I cannot bring my family their food."

"We *have* to eat in the assembly halls."

Mother rubbed my father's shoulders. He put his hands on hers.

"Father, I think you're the cat's meow."

"I am not the only man who feels this way."

Mother spoke softly. "We do not blame you for the way we live."

"We should have left with Toshio." Father looked angry. "I thought America was the place to raise my family—to spare my children the ugliness of life. I was wrong." Father swallowed. "I am sorry I did not listen to Margaret." He touched my cheek.

I choked my sorrow. For the first time, my father spoke of this country negatively. "We'll return to our lives when the war is over."

Father clutched my hand. "You make me feel better. Good night." He went behind the curtain to my parents' cot.

I sat on the porch, wondering where John was, what he was doing. I closed my eyes and imagined him beside me, wanting him close. A deadly noise erupted from the neighboring apartments, jolting me from my dream. I quickly tiptoed to the corner of our barracks and peeked around.

"You don't belong here."

"Leave our girls alone."

A group of teenagers was yelling at a white man married to a Nisei woman. It was the same man I had spoken to our first week in the camp. I started to slip back into the shadows, then remembered how Mrs. Grady rescued me from those hoods in the school hallway. I clutched John's ring, quelling my fear. I elbowed my way through the crowd and stood in front of the man. "Scram!"

"Get a wiggle on, white lover," one of the group yelled at me.

I noticed Timmy on the fringe of the gang. My stomach dropped. Which side would he choose? I set my jaw. "What did this man do to you?"

"He doesn't belong here!"

"Neither do we."

"He shouldn't be with our women."

"He's here with his wife and his children. His family. Go home to your families."

"Come on," Timmy said to the leader. "Let's go."

I edged back to my cot. Using a candle, I wrote, with a shaky hand, in my diary.

Timmy's battling to find his place. He's restless. Now that Robert's married, Timmy's lost. Most of the boys his age idolize and imitate the teenagers. Unfortunately, most of them are hooligans. They stalk around the camp, starting fights and taunting the older people. It's like the camp gives them power to do whatever they want. Unless the gangs become violent, the guards rarely do anything about them.

In November, I penned an editorial for the camp paper.

Our situation seems so bleak. We have no rules to follow, except that we cannot go out of the gates. Some internees have jobs and are grateful for them. Very few kids over 16 returned to school and have nothing to occupy their time. The elderly can't help their families in the ways they have for years. Those without jobs or duties wander aimlessly, expected to be content to be fed three times a day and share a group bathroom. We can do anything but leave.

The days started getting colder. We pulled out our jackets and wore them to keep the chill off. Our weather changed from melting hot to icicle cold. By the middle of November, resentments about camp life exploded in Poston.

"Last night, the doctors worked on a man who was almost beaten to death," Robert told us at breakfast.

"Why?" I asked, reaching for my notebook.

"He was suspected of being an informant for the camp administrators."

"Is he going to live?" I asked.

Robert nodded. "Parents of another suspected informant were also beaten."

"To force the informant to stop." I scribbled down information as fast as I could. Informants were called inu, which meant dog.

Protests and strikes divided the camp into those sympathetic to the suspected informants and those sympathetic to the accused assailants. It was a weekly problem. One morning, my stomach flip-flopped as soldiers marched to the gates, guns drawn.

"They're actually going to shoot?" I said softly.

"I hope they do," Timmy said.

"People could be killed!"

"People are killed every day in the war. At least it would be some excitement."

An actual fight was diverted. At that point, I knew living in the camp was more dangerous than living outside as long as the gangs roamed.

Our camp had self-government, with block representatives. They formed community councils. Only the Nisei, or American-born Japanese, could serve on the councils, but everyone over sixteen could vote. For some Japanese-born, like my parents, it was the first American election in which they had voted. Robert was selected to be a block representative.

Camp disputes were settled by judicial committees, made up of three Nisei and three whites, all chosen by the camp director. Councils and committees had no decision-making power. That, plus the Nisei stipulation, caused resentment and mistrust among internees. The older generation resented their children making the decisions and serving on councils, while those on the committees felt powerless to change their situation. Each day, hatred spread among the people living in our camp.

"Why are you on the committee?" Father asked Robert.

"I was born in America."

"Elders should be leaders."

"That's an old-fashioned belief, Father. It simply isn't possible in the camp."

"Born in America did not keep you out of the camp." Father retreated to his apartment and left Robert sitting on the porch.

I attended council meetings and reported in our camp paper. My reports had to be approved by the camp directors before I could print them.

The grade school children presented a holiday pageant, providing a pleasant diversion from camp life. The littlest children dressed as pilgrims and Indians. I had much to be thankful for, most especially my family. During the pageant, Nancy placed my hand on her belly. I felt a rippling across her stomach. "The baby?"

Her face was a mixture of joy and relief. "I hadn't felt it move yet."

Something changed in my father's eyes. Instead of the guarded look he had worn since the baby's announcement, he seemed pleased. I smiled, knowing this baby would unite everyone.

I received a letter from John on the day before Thanksgiving. It had been opened and read by the guard, which instantly infuriated me. It was *my* letter. The guard had read private things John had intended for me. John's handwriting made me feel closer to him and made me miss him all the more. The guard had blackened out the last two lines of the letter. I'm sure John had told me that he loved me.

My eyes filled with tears, feeling cheated out of those words. Just reading his words made me want to touch him, to kiss him. I had feared, while he was gone, my longing for him would decrease. But it didn't. I was also afraid he'd stop loving me. That he would join his bunkies on their R and R exploits.

I wrote to him about Sharon Ito and our new friendship. I told him about Robert and Nancy and the baby coming. Maybe because of Nancy, I often thought about John and whether we had a future together. I had to plan my own future and hope John would come home to be part of it.

CHAPTER 26
Holiday Time

Several thousand of us crowded into the mess halls for Thanksgiving. I thought of our house in Valle Verde. Mother, Barbara, and I would have made a huge dinner. Uncle Toshio's family would have shared our feast. The Wilsons and Satos would have joined us for dessert.

"Do you think they'll fix us turkey?" Timmy asked.

"It wouldn't be Thanksgiving without it," I said.

I looked at my plate as my meal was dished. "Creamed turkey?" I wanted to cry. "What are the green lumps?"

"That's our salad," Robert laughed and nudged my shoulder.

Giggling, I forced my throat to swallow, then pushed my plate away.

"I've definitely eaten better," Robert said.

"I've lost weight since we've been here," I said. "The food is so disgusting."

December meant freezing weather. I never would have believed a desert could be absolute hell in the winter. It was so cold my family started using a chamber pot at night, rather than running to the common bathroom. The pot worked until Timmy got the flu.

"I've got to heave!" he cried and headed for the bathroom. Father rose.

"You stay in bed." I hurried after Timmy, wrapping my coat around me. I held his forehead as he puked, urging myself to keep my own cookies down.

"Are you feeling any better, Timmy?" I asked as I wiped his face off.

Timmy shrugged.

"Let's get back to the room. I'm freezing."

"Go back yourself." He lay on the cold floor.

"Not without you. Then Father would come." I sat down on a toilet seat, hugging my knees to my chin.

"I don't need any of you in here with me." Timmy stormed out of the bathroom. He was twelve. He wanted to start breaking away from the family more, but still needed us. My parents were afraid the gangs would swoop down and lure him in.

I took a deep breath and charged after Timmy. He wasn't my annoying little brother any longer. He was a drone who lashed out at everyone around him.

"Do you want to talk?" I asked one morning on the way to school.

"I wouldn't talk to you—you neck with white boys."

"Timmy!"

"It's true. You should stick to our kind."

"What's *our* kind?"

"Japanese. The whites don't like us. John's just using you."

"What's he using me for?"

"White guys think Jap women are dainty. He'll monk all he wants in the war."

I yanked Timmy around to face me. He was my height, and I looked into his eyes. "Don't talk to me like that. You idolized John. He loves you like a brother."

Timmy shrugged. "I know what's going on."

"You don't!" I screamed and slapped him.

He stumbled to school, and I felt sick. My parents could try to protect him, but the gangs had gotten Timmy. He had known John all his life, and now he thought John was evil. Timmy was turning away from his family.

During the holidays, the mood of the camp was one of disbelief and despair. The fence surrounding the camp represented the line we couldn't cross. That fence was protecting the rest of the country from us. That fence denied us freedom.

One afternoon, I noticed some four-year-old girls playing "house." Instead of fixing meals and rocking dolls, these girls lined up to eat in a mess hall. They pretended their husbands sat around all day in a camp. I hurried to my typewriter:

> *Just because we were placed inside this camp, behind this wire, doesn't mean we should let our families deteriorate. The camp is making us dependent on the government. Parents aren't disciplining their children. More and more kids are getting into trouble. Before the war, juvenile delinquency among Japanese Americans was practically nonexistent. With the collapse of a strong family, delinquency and related problems are rampant in the camp. It's hard to retain the family, but one day, we're going to be released from the camp. Then what?*

That evening, at supper, I peeked around. "Most of the kids do eat with their friends, rather than with family. If we were at home, Timmy would be sitting with us."

"Parents are losing control," Mother said. "We have lost Timmy."

"He does not respect the family," Father agreed.

Gang numbers were increasing—boys old enough to abstain from school were angry, resentful. They roamed day and night, goading people into fights.

I fed Audrey some of my dinner. Her smile was contagious, and soon I grinned at her, but I overheard conversations.

"You must stop carousing with the men. It is not proper."

"Quit batting your gums, Mama. It isn't proper to be in this camp, either."

"Why do you talk so to me?"

"Because you have no power over me. It's your fault I'm here, not mine."

Some Issei resented their own children. On the outside, elders made decisions, and children obeyed. In camp, the Nisei made decisions. I could never lose respect for my parents. I disagreed with them sometimes, but they were good people. Some Nisei were disrespectful toward their parents. I didn't want the responsibility of making decisions for our family, but more and more, my father was turning to me for answers. I wanted things the way they were before the war.

My birthday came and went. I didn't want a party—it would remind me too much of last year's and my time with John. Had it only been one year since he first kissed me? He sent me a simple card.

"We'll celebrate all the lost holidays as soon as I get home," it said.

There was also a small box; I tore it open, anxious to see what he had sent me.

Thought you might enjoy.

Inside the box was a toy necklace, made from thin metal. When I lifted the necklace, the cotton fell out. In the very center of the cotton was a small lump. I dug it out and found a scrap of paper. Hidden inside was a single pearl.

For my pearl. You deserve so much more.

I ached for him. I wanted to kiss him, like we had on my sixteenth birthday. And smooch. I wanted to hold John, naked, our bodies pressed together. To keep from going crazy, I studied with Sharon Ito.

"Can I see a picture of your John?" Sharon asked.

"I haven't shown him to you?" I reached for my small handbag and handed his often-held picture to Sharon.

"He's so dreamy!" Sharon sighed. "No wonder you're in love with him."

My cheeks grew hot. Was it that obvious? "Do you have a boyfriend?"

Sharon shook her head. "Never been kissed. Although, if someone swoony like John is waiting for me, I'll be more patient."

Dear Diary,

Sharon and I giggle together a lot. It's fun to share my feelings with someone who isn't so involved in my history. She makes me feel better about missing John so much. And she makes me realize I have to be more honest with my parents about my feelings for John.

As Christmas approached, my family had a meeting. Father spoke softly. "I do not think we celebrate any more holidays until the war is over."

"Until we can all be together again," Mother said.

"I love John," I admitted to my parents.

"He is a good son," my father said. "We have always liked John Wilson."

"I want him to come back safely."

"He will." Father patted my arm.

Dear Diary,

Will I be strong enough to go on if John is killed? I want to believe John will come home. But my father told us America would take care of us. I guess he was right. America did take care of us, just not in the way my father believed. Is he wrong about John's coming home safely too?

CHAPTER 27
Loyalty

In January, the War Department circulated the loyalty questionnaire to all Japanese Americans seventeen and older. Father, Mother, Robert, and I had to answer the questions. There were two questions on the form that disturbed me, numbers 27 and 28. For the men, it read:

No. 27. Are you willing to serve in the armed forces of the United States on combat duty wherever ordered?
No. 28. Will you swear unqualified allegiance to the United States of America and faithfully defend the United States from any or all attack by foreign or domestic forces, and forswear any form of allegiance or obedience to the Japanese emperor, to any other foreign government, power or organization?

For the women, question 27 asked if we would be willing to volunteer for the Army Nurse Corps or Women's Army Corps. Question 28 omitted any reference to defending the country. The questionnaires had to be answered in front of army recruiters; so once again, we stood in lines. We tried to keep warm by stamping our feet and standing close. This issue of loyalty divided our camp.

"We are not eligible for citizenship in the United States," an Issei woman said. "What happens if we renounce Japan, where we are allowed to be citizens?"

"We could end up stateless people," her husband said.

Hurt and confusion showed on the faces of the elderly. But my father's deep-rooted belief in America allowed him to answer only yes to the question of allegiance. "This is my only way to show I am an American," Father said. "Even if America does not allow me to be a citizen."

"I shouldn't have to renounce Japan," I said. "I've never been to that country."

"It does not make sense," Father agreed.

"I'm an American citizen, aren't I?" I gritted my teeth. "How can I give up allegiance to a country that means nothing to me?"

"I'm with you," Robert said. "Our generation, born in the United States, is asked to prove our loyalty above and beyond other Americans."

I looked at the pride in Robert's face. Now he could stand up and say he was an American, to the army—the very group that didn't want him after Pearl Harbor.

Several in front of us refused to answer the questions. They stared straight ahead, ignoring the recruiters. After several tense minutes, they were led away. Some answered no to both questions. They were labeled the "no-nos." They scared me. They had nothing left except hatred. Many of the no-nos were the older boys that had formed the gangs. I knew if Timmy were old enough to answer, his response would be "no-no."

The man in front of me answered yes-yes. "Am I an American?" he asked.

The recruiter nodded absently.

"May I go to Tucson?"

"That's part of the restricted area," the recruiter answered.

The man reached for his questionnaire, tore it up, and left the line.

Everyone in our family answered yes to both questions. I felt a surge of hope. By answering in the positive maybe our time in camp was winding down.

Strolling back to our apartment, I noticed Timmy crouched down by the garden. He was smoking!

"Where did you get that?" I demanded.

"What's it to you?"

"You're not old enough to be smoking."

"I'm old enough for a lot of things."

On January 28, restrictions on Nisei service were removed. Nisei men could now enlist in the armed forces. Nancy ran to our room.

"Margaret, you've got to talk to him."

"Who?" I asked.

"Calm him down." Nancy was seven months pregnant and having a harder time breathing. "He wants to enlist. The idiot wants to join the army!"

"Who?" I asked again, grabbing Nancy's shoulders.

"Robert."

I looked up as Robert rounded the corner.

"Nancy, please don't run away from me," Robert screamed. "I have to join."

"They didn't want you in the army. They put you in a concentration camp. Why would you fight their war?" Nancy sobbed on my shoulder.

I wanted to leave them alone, but didn't dare move.

"This is the chance to prove we're loyal. Maybe by my fighting, we can go home." Robert squatted down and put his hand on Nancy's knee. "I have to do this."

Nancy continued crying as my parents returned from lunch.

"What is wrong?" Father asked, alarmed. "Nancy? The baby?"

Robert stood. "I've decided to enlist in the army. And that has upset my wife."

I grabbed Robert's arm with my free hand. He clutched my fingers and clenched his jaw. His wanting to fight now wasn't the same as a year ago. Then, he wanted revenge. Now, with a wife and baby coming, it was duty.

"I am proud of your decision, my son." Father clasped both of Robert's shoulders. "A fine way to prove the family's allegiance."

Robert relaxed. I felt the tension leave his hand.

"We just got married," Nancy said softly. She touched her stomach, then looked at my father. "You'd send your son off to be killed in a war that we've already lost?"

"What do you mean, Nancy?" I asked. I pushed the hair out of her eyes.

"America doesn't care about us. They're treating us like the enemy. They're going to use us to fight the war. They're going to take sons and husbands out of the camps and let them be killed."

"I don't think that's the way to look at it." I felt a pang of empathy for her.

"John's already fighting. Chances are, he won't come back."

My head snapped back in reaction to Nancy's comment.

"I'm sorry, Margaret. I didn't mean that." Nancy grabbed my arm as I stood up. I broke free and bolted away from her. Nancy was right. Chances were, John wouldn't come home. I had to start thinking in those terms, to keep from going crazy with worry. All these months I was convinced I needed John in order for my life to have meaning. Suddenly, I knew I had to have meaning for myself. John couldn't provide that for me.

I wandered around for hours, thinking about loyalty. How could I prove myself loyal? I decided all I could do was the best job possible to help my family. I felt a sudden release of some inner burden I didn't realize I had. I felt lighter, knowing I couldn't change the course of the war or the consequences of it. All I could do was be strong for my parents, as they had always been for me. The best way I could help was to continue working on the camp paper and pray that all those I loved would be kept safe. I sat in the mess hall and scribbled down my next editorial:

>   *How do we, as Japanese immigrants and their children, prove loyalty to a country that doesn't trust us, simply because of where our ancestors were born? This war has taught me loyalty is more than proving yourself worthy to America. Loyalty is in your heart. My father has shown me this many times since the war started. We can't, beyond any doubt, prove ourselves to this government. We can satisfy our own criteria for loyalty. None of us should be in this camp. We are being detained by prejudice. I'm going to build on the person I already am. I am worthy of a better life and someday, I'll make that a reality. For now, I'll do what I can to make life in camp as bearable as possible.*

When I returned to our room, the Satos were there for their daily cup of tea.

"I heard the government is disappointed in the number of volunteers. Many of the young men are angry and refuse to fight in the war." Mrs. Sato spoke so softly, I had to actually put my ear toward her.

Nancy looked at Robert, and tears filled her eyes. My stomach knotted.

On February 4, 1943, the army activated the 442nd Regimental Combat Team, composed of the 100th Battalion from Hawaii and volunteers from the camps. Robert was selected to serve in the combat team. It was an all-Nisei unit of six thousand men.

I asked him quietly. "Do you think you'll fight against any of our family?" We had lots of cousins in Japan that we had never seen, many of them our ages.

Robert's mouth dropped open. "Anyone in a Japanese uniform is the enemy."

During the next few days, I thought about my childhood and my big brother.

Dear Diary,

As Robert prepares to leave, I prepare myself to be as brave as he is. My heart is breaking at the thought of his leaving our family. He's one of my best friends. I've had so much fun working with him on the paper. He's the first to cheer me up about John. I don't want him to go, but I understand how important it is for him to do this. Now, I have to be the strong one, not only for my parents, but for Nancy too. And hope that God will keep him and John safe.

On the day he shipped out, everyone cried, including Robert.

"I know I'm doing the right thing," Robert said. Was he trying to convince himself? The rest of us?

I hugged him tight. "I love you."

"Take care of Mom and Dad while I'm away."

Nancy grabbed Robert. "Don't get yourself killed," she sobbed. "Come back. The baby . . ."

Robert touched her stomach. "I don't want to die." Robert kissed her, then went through the gate to board a bus bound for basic training in Camp Shelby, Mississippi. Nancy clung to me as she wept. A single, silent tear rolled down my cheek.

Two of the men I loved most in the world had left me standing at a gate. Would they return to me?

CHAPTER 28
New Beginnings

For the next six weeks, Nancy and I drew closer again.

"Now I know what it's like to stay close through letters," Nancy said.

"I write letters to John all the time, and I never know whether he's really getting them."

Dear Diary,

I'm at peace now that I've decided my own life is enough for me. I love John more than I thought possible to love another person. But I'm finally learning to love myself. If John dies, I have to be able to live. If he comes home to me, my life will be divine. But without him, I will still have worth.

Nancy pined away for Robert. If not for the baby, she might have simply stopped eating. Elizabeth had been sending fresh fruit each month. Even though the guards took the best of it, it tasted luscious. Elizabeth kept me informed about high school, but I felt ten years older than anyone in Valle Verde High School.

At the end of March, right on her due date, Nancy gave birth. Terrified, I stayed with her. I kept remembering how Barbara had bled to death in Salinas.

158

"You can do it, Nancy," I said. "Think of Robert."

"Futz!" Nancy screamed as she struggled through contractions. "It's too hard."

"I'm right here," I assured her.

"It hurts!" Nancy cried, thrashing around. Her movements proved to me she was stronger than Barbara had been.

"When this is over, you'll have Robert's baby," I said as I wiped her forehead.

After seventeen hours of labor, Nancy gave birth to a boy. He was small, which probably helped her deliver him without any complications. As she held her son, I sponged her face. "I'm proud of you, doll."

"It *is* labor."

"I don't know if I'll be able to do this," I confessed.

"Lamb pie, you're so brave. This will be a cinch for you."

"I'm not brave, Nancy. I'm so scared most of the time, I just react."

"You can't fool me." She tried to nurse my nephew, but he wasn't interested. "You're an amazing friend."

I touched the baby's cheek and smiled. "What are you going to name him?"

"Joshua Robert Yamaguchi. What do you think?"

"Oolie droolie," I sighed. "He's perfect."

"I wish Robert was here." Nancy bit her lip.

"Do you want me to take Joshua, so you can sleep?" I scooped up Joshua as Nancy closed her eyes. "You *are* okay? You're not going to fade away on me like . . ." I couldn't finish the sentence.

"I'm just tired. The doctor said I'm fine. And at least there's a hospital here." She put her hand over mine. "Thanks."

I rocked the warm baby in my arms and watched my friend sleep. I was the happiest I had been in months. I couldn't wait to tell John that Robert and Nancy had a son! We all seemed so much older. We should have been necking in parked cars. Instead, we were fighting wars and having babies while we were teenagers. I walked to the waiting area, so the family could see the newest addition. "This is Joshua."

Mrs. Sato snatched him away first. The looks on the faces of all four grandparents were ones of instant love.

"I can see this one won't be spoiled," I said sarcastically.

Mother swatted at me playfully. "He is beautiful. Nancy is resting?"

"Our daughter? . . ." Mr. Sato asked.

"She's sleeping."

Mr. Sato put his arm around his wife and gazed at his new grandson.

I sat beside my mother and took her hands. "Mother, I just want to thank you—I took so much for granted."

"We all did."

I cuddled Audrey as everyone passed Joshua around. Audrey was almost a year old. She tried to pull herself up and walk. I grabbed her pudgy hands and steadied her. She yawned, making me sleepy. I was relieved Nancy and the baby were okay, but I was exhausted.

"I'm going to take Audrey to Howard." I carried Audrey. Soon, her little head was nestled in my neck, and I hugged her tight. As I took Audrey back to Howard's room, I thought about school. I would graduate at the end of the school year. I was seventeen and ready for a new challenge. I had to admit, school had been very easy this past year, even though I took senior classes. I decided to apply to colleges.

I spotted Timmy smoking again, this time with a bottle of beer in his hand. I avoided him, slipping into the shadows with Audrey.

The next week, Sharon Ito and I studied for a history test.

"I've really enjoyed spending time with you," Sharon said. "It's hard for me to meet new people."

"Me too," I said. "I've always been bashful."

"You don't seem shy, Margaret. You've done so much in this camp. The weekly dances lift everyone's spirits. And the paper—I don't know how you do it."

"My brother Robert helped me with the paper."

"Are you doing it by yourself now?"

"The layout isn't as good as it was when he helped, but I don't have any choice."

"Can I help?"

"That would be the bee's knees!"

During April and May, Sharon and I worked together on the paper, and I felt more like a high school kid than a deb in an internment camp.

"Do you think Philip Yoshihiro likes me?" Sharon asked.

"Likes you? He thinks you're *it*!" I squealed.

Sharon giggled. "He's cute, don't you think?"

"He's a sugarpuss."

I hadn't realized until Sharon and I started giggling over silly things that Nancy and I hadn't been goofy together for over a year.

Dear Diary,

All my life, Nancy has been my closest friend. I was always content having one good friend. Until now. In a way, Nancy has given me a gift—I can survive without her in my daily life. She'll always be my friend, but she's shut part of her life off from me. Part of me resents that.

After all, growing up, Nancy has always been the playful, flirting one. She always had lots of friends—boys and girls. I had always felt privileged she chose me to be her best friend. But as a result, I didn't make many other close friends. Now, I'm free to branch out and find my own way. I'm not stuck in her shadow. I'm my own person. I like me.

"Let's do a formal dance," I said to Sharon. "To end the school year right."

Mother helped me make a dress out of some pale green satin. "I have had this fabric for a long time."

"What for?"

"It would have made a lovely prom dress." She fitted me and we cut the fabric into pieces. It was a simple design. The dress was formfitting, with thin straps. Mother made a wrap for around my shoulders and a ribbon for my hair.

On the night of the dance, Sharon and I did each other's hair. "It's fun to dress up, even if my guy is a world away," I said. I dolled up my dress with my pearl pin and the earrings from John. Even though the heavy chain didn't exactly go with the elegance of the dress, I proudly wore John's ring. I felt like a princess, waiting for my handsome prince to come rescue me from a horrible fate.

Philip asked Sharon to dance, and they spent the rest of the evening in each other's arms. I danced a few times, but enjoyed scribbling in my notebook.

> *Couples are forming on the dance floor. Some of the debs are even boodling with the guards. Unplanned pregnancies have erupted in the camp. Everyone feels desperate. If we were still in our homes and schools, most kids wouldn't be fooling around. But here, the rules have shifted. We aren't treated the same here as we were in our schools. The guards view us as animals or possessions. There are times I want to feel like my old self.*
>
> *I know if John were here, I'd want to kiss him and touch him until I felt human.*

In June, Sharon and I planned a summer fun issue of the camp paper.

"This layout is great," I said. "I like the way you used the headlines in an image."

"You don't think it's stupid?"

"You're a natural artist."

"My parents want me to choose a 'real' job skill," Sharon admitted.

I squeezed her hand. "Don't give up, if it's your dream."

Dear Diary,

Sharon has changed as she's worked on the paper. Everyone in camp reads it and it actually affects people's opinions of what's happening in the world. She's feeling more confident in her abilities. She's a divine artist.

By July, Joshua was fat and happy. Nancy was a dutiful and doting mother. She had a knack for it I never would have guessed. Maybe when it was yours and someone you loved, it made a difference.

I received letters from John and Robert. John had kept his promise of not telling me where he was, but I hadn't requested that from Robert.

Dear Mar,

We fought with the 100th Infantry Battalion in Italy, France, and Germany. It's nasty fighting, Sis. But if this will prove my loyalty—our family's loyalty—it's worth it to me. Tell Mom and Dad I said hello. And thanks for helping Nancy. With me over here, you're her world. I'm proud of you, Margaret.

Love you,
Robert

Robert had sent a picture of himself in uniform. He looked like a man.

Dear Diary,

As the summer blossoms, so does Father's garden. He whistles as he weeds and waters the growing plants. Mother works outside also, just not as quickly or as long as she had before. My parents are aging, much faster than they should be. The one thing they haven't relinquished is their dignity. I'm proud that despite the disgraces they have to live with, they hold their heads high. They make me determined to do the same.

Timmy turned thirteen and was the only thorn in our family. I prayed for him each day, hoping he would settle down. But the influence of the gang members swayed him. He spoke rudely to everyone and stayed out late at night.

"Where have you been?" I asked him at midnight.

"What's it to you?" Timmy snarled.

"I care about you. Please stop hanging around those boys."

"Dry up." Timmy shoved me hard, and I fell off the little porch outside our room. He stomped into the barracks and let the door slam.

I sat on the dirt and cried. I was scared of my little brother! I wouldn't give up on him, but I wouldn't allow him to hurt us. Maybe all I could do was pray for him. I certainly was no match for him physically.

Summer blossomed as Howard drowned in his grief. He looked like he had aged about ten years. But he adored Audrey. I watched her almost every day while he napped, and I fell completely head over heels in love with her. She teetered and tried to talk.

Her first word was "annee."

"What an honor," Mother said.

"You are indeed a special person to her," Father said.

I hugged Audrey and twirled with her. "Yes, I'm your Auntie Mar."

The camp seemed to have an upbeat attitude during the summer. The army was allowing in Japanese Americans. Those Nisei that served were proving their patriotism by fighting with honor. In August, I wrote an editorial for the paper:

> *Could this be our last summer in this camp? The Nisei men can volunteer to serve in the armed forces. This can only mean the government is admitting its error. The momentum of the war seems to be in America's favor. Let's hope it is. I'm ready to return to the life I had before the war started. As summer closes, I'm left with one thought: Home.*

CHAPTER 29
Death

As the months passed into one another, the older generation began to lose faith in what lay ahead for them.

"Mother, Mrs. Hirosho died."

"She was very old," Mother said. "So much change. So much sadness."

"She was such a sweet lady," I said.

"She died of old age and uselessness."

I thought it was shame and boredom that made many of the older generation give up and die.

My father's faith steadily unraveled. "I thought this would be settled by now," Father said one evening. "That America would see it was wrong for putting its people in camps. I can understand why they put the Issei in. But why you? Why the Nisei? You are citizens. Should that not have counted for something?"

I shrugged my shoulders. "I wouldn't have stayed knowing you had to be in a camp. We're together. That's what matters."

Summer turned to fall and fall to winter—monotonous months full of mundane apathy. My hope of being released from the camp now seemed absurd. We were left in limbo, abandoned by America. I tried to remain positive, but it became more difficult each day, especially when surrounded by gloom and doom.

"Nancy," I said, "are you coming to dinner with us?"

"No. Would you take Joshua?" She handed over her son.

"Again? Aren't you going to eat?"

"I'm not hungry. I think I'll lie down awhile."

"You've been napping all day," I argued.

"Just take him," Nancy snapped.

I packed Joshua to the mess hall while Audrey toddled beside me. We all missed Robert, and my heart ached for John. But I showed a happy face to everyone. I figured if I appeared cheerful on the outside, I'd feel better on the inside.

In the mess hall, I listened to people who lived around me.

"In another few years, we'll have a wonderful garden growing behind our block," one man said to his wife.

"My son says after he finishes high school, he will apply for college mail courses," a lady said. I glanced at her son; he was about Timmy's age.

"Why should we work?" a man in his thirties said. "We're provided our meals. There really isn't much we can buy."

"That's right," his friend said. "And we're not paid fairly."

Older people simply sat and let the days filter by them. I was determined not to become so melancholy. I began a correspondence college course in secretarial skills.

Dear Diary,

This isn't what I ultimately want, but there aren't many college programs offered to camp internees. I figure the skills will at least get me a job once the war was over. I won't surrender myself to this camp!

I continued printing the paper and felt at ease, amid the angry resentment emanating throughout the camp. We repeated another holiday season in the camp, praying for an end to the war and a return of our loved ones.

In January 1944, it was announced that Japanese Americans were eligible for the draft. Now it was the government's *right* to make Japanese American men fight, versus *allowing* Nisei men to enlist.

"This means we should go home," I said excitedly.

Father stared out the door and shrugged his shoulders. His eyes looked dull and his face weathered.

But we didn't leave the camp. My heart sank.

Dear Diary,

Maybe Nancy was right all along. Maybe the government is just raiding the camps. Maybe it thinks we're expendable. How long can this damned war go on? How long can we be expected to live like this? Will Audrey and Joshua grow up living like criminals?

Howard was drafted in February. He gave temporary custody of Audrey to me.

"In case I don't come back," he said.

"You'll be back."

Howard's eyes made me uneasy. I hastily scribbled a note to John.

Dear John,

Howard was drafted and asked if I would take custody of Audrey if anything happened to him. Am I crazy?

I love you.

Mar

A month later, I received his answer.

Dear Margaret,

You are a loving, generous woman. You eased Howard's mind about Audrey. I bet she's beautiful. If something happens to Howard, we'll take care of her.

I love you.

John

That letter did more for my faith than anything. John called me a woman! Not a girl or young lady. A woman. I was feeling more like a woman all the time. And he said, *we'll* take care of Audrey. For the rest of the day, my smiles were genuine.

In June 1944, my family received two telegrams from the U.S. Army. The first one said that Howard had been killed in combat. Because his parents were already dead, we were the only family he had left.

"Howard," I whispered and cried warm, silent tears. "He'll never see his daughter grow up." Then a flood of emotions broke loose in my chest. "Poor Audrey!" She'll meet her parents and learn about them through pictures and stories we tell her.

"Our family is shrinking," Mother said sadly.

The full effect of Howard's death hit me as my mother handed me Audrey.

"Can I do this?" I asked my mother. "Can I be a mother?"

"You are a good parent, already, Daughter." She held my chin in her hand. "You are loving but firm with Audrey. Howard knew what he was doing."

"Do you think he wanted to die in the war?" I whispered.

"I do not think he ever got over Barbara's death. He felt at fault."

"Like, if they had been at home, he would have taken her to the hospital?"

"He could not insist on that in the assembly center."

We cried for Howard's death, but he had seemed almost dead for so long, it was a relief that his suffering had ended. "You're back with your love, Howard," I whispered that night in my prayers.

The very next day, another telegram arrived. When I saw the courier approach our apartment, my body froze. Was it John or Robert?

I screamed. "No!"

Mother and Father ran outside, saw the man, and both of them knew someone had died. Mother took my hands, and we stood as Father read the telegram. I studied his face but couldn't read it. What was in the telegram?

"Father?" I asked, touching his arm.

He stood motionless. My heart thumped inside my chest. It seemed hours went by without a sound from my father.

"Tamaki," Mother urged. "What is in the letter?"

"Our son is dead," Father said quietly.

I felt as if my body were splitting in two. I shook my head from side to side. "No, it can't be true."

Mother sank to the ground. I knelt beside her and lifted her into my arms. I carried my mother to our room, amazed at how light she was. I glanced at Timmy; he sat on the floor, staring straight ahead.

"Timmy," I said gently. "We found out some bad news."

"Robert's dead." He sat beside Mother.

Was he so far detached, Robert's death meant nothing? Another hole in my heart tore open at the thought of it. "Would you stay with Mother? Father and I have to tell Nancy."

"Shove in your clutch," Timmy said, dragging on his cigarette. He held Mother's hand, but that was the only reaction I saw from him.

Father and I walked in silence to Nancy's room. My chest ached from restrained sobs. I had to get this over with so I could let myself cry. There was no one to comfort me; I just wanted to let it all out before I exploded.

We arrived at Nancy's to find her parents there, helping her with Joshua.

"Nancy," Father said. "Please sit down."

Nancy's face paled to white. "It's Robert, isn't it?"

My father nodded.

Nancy started to shake. "He can't be dead. I got a letter from him just today."

Mrs. Sato grabbed her daughter as a sob escaped from her mouth.

"I am sorry," Mr. Sato said. "He was a good boy."

"A good boy?" Nancy repeated, then started laughing. "A good boy? I know you've resented him knocking me up, Daddy. But we loved each other."

I put my arms around my friend and felt her tremble. Nancy looked at me. I thought she was going to lash out, then she stopped. "He never got to see his son."

We wept together for most of the night. Our bodies racked with sobs as we said goodbye to the one man we both loved. The strongest connection between us was now gone.

"Did he know I loved him?" Nancy wailed. "Did he really know it?"

"He knew, doll."

As morning began, there was no moisture left in our bodies. I rested my head on Nancy's shoulder and watched the sunrise.

CHAPTER 30
Hope

During the next six months, my connection with John seemed so fragile. I waited every day for his letters, which came almost every day. Then one day, I heard nothing. No letter arrived for a week. I stopped eating. I stopped sleeping. I knew John was dead. The courier came with a telegram. But he walked past our room to the folks next door. I breathed a sigh of relief, then instantly felt guilty. Those people had an only son who had volunteered with Robert.

Finally, I received another letter.

Dear Margaret,

My sweet pearl. Thank you for all the sugar reports. I'm sorry I haven't sent any letters. I feel like a drip. We ended up moving and I couldn't manage postal service. I miss you so much, it hurts. Living with a bunch of crude, smelly men is all wet! I'd much rather be living with warm, sweet you, if you'll have me when this is over. Marry me?

Thinking about you is the only thing keeping me from going AWOL. I'm not cut out for army life. Especially not for the life of a grunt. How's Audrey? And little Joshua. It hasn't sunk in yet how much our lives have changed

*because of this damned war. I can't really believe Robert is
dead. He's been my best friend for so long. It's like losing a
brother.*

Remember, I love you, and try not to worry.
John

John wanted to marry me! I hugged the letter to my chest
and screamed, "Yes." I loved John more than ever. He still
loved me!

Dear Diary,

*I try hard not to worry about John, but I know he could
be killed at any moment. It's a balancing act for me to go on
each day. I work on the paper, keep Nancy company, and
take care of Audrey. I'm a mother! It really isn't that much
different from when Howard was still with us. I just try to
stay as busy as I can, so I can't think too much of how
much danger John's in. And then there's Timmy. I want to
help my parents with him, but they can't seem to do anything. Except love him. Timmy is going deeper into the gangs.
We're losing him. We're losing Nancy too. There isn't any
joy left in her. She's so depressed. I don't think she even
wants to take care of sweet little Joshua. What abominable
events this war has caused.*

Walking back from lunch one day, I confided, "Mother, I'm
so scared. John wants to get married. What if he doesn't come
back?"

"You must have faith. It will turn out the way it is supposed
to."

"You've lost a daughter and a son because of this war."

"Perhaps it is the way our life was fated. If, in the long run,
it means peace and freedom, I will not be bitter."

"You are amazing, Mother. I love you."

"And I love you. It is time for me to rest."

I kissed my mother, then took Audrey to Nancy's room to
play with Joshua. The kids scooted around the floor as I

sketched them. I saw life and hope and energy in their eyes. It radiated from their bodies and infected me. I related more to the children than to the rest of my family. I wanted to move and do things. Everyone around me was slowing down.

Nancy napped constantly. Mother had started resting after lunch. And Father sat in his chair in the afternoons and closed his eyes.

After Nancy woke, Audrey and I returned to find my mother on the floor.

"Mother!" I screamed. "Wake up."

Father ran into the room. "Not my wife." He scooped Mother up and ran to the hospital with her.

The doctor shook his head. "I'm sorry. She probably died instantly, an embolism. She didn't suffer."

I covered my mouth with my hand. Did she know how much I loved her? Another chunk of my heart shredded. "May we see her?" Time was suspended. I crept to her bedside like I was moving through sludge.

Audrey kept saying, "Grammie, Grammie, where are you?" I left her in the nursery while I made peace with death, again.

"Goodbye, Mother. I love you." I stroked her hand and pushed the hair from her face. Lying on the cot, she looked tiny. Her clothes seemed huge. I never realized how little she really was. I kissed her forehead and left my father alone with her.

I heard him speaking softly, first in English then a few words in Japanese. I was shocked. He hadn't spoken the language for years. It scared me to hear him lapse into the enemy's language. Had anyone heard him?

While I waited for him, I replayed the afternoon in my head. Nothing was different from any other day. Except Mother never woke from her nap. I felt numb. My arms and legs were weighted down. I couldn't possibly absorb any more grief.

I thought back to our life in Valle Verde, to the fights Mother and I had. Such stupid arguments. Such trivial things to quarrel about. I was ashamed of how I had acted toward my mother in that life.

Father stepped from the cot and put his hands over his face. I grasped his shoulders and guided him toward our room. We trudged home in silence. Once on the porch, I took his hand and felt it tremble. He clutched me hard and sobbed. "My beautiful bride is gone now."

I comforted him like he was a child. "It will be okay, Father. I'm still here. And Timmy. Audrey."

"No, daughter. My life is over. My half is not complete."

I had never heard my father cry before. I wept with him until Timmy showed up, late that night.

"Mother died today." I didn't feel generous toward my little brother. He hadn't been around all day, and I didn't care if the news hurt him.

Timmy looked like I had hit him. "She died?" He sunk down on the porch. I returned to our room, to be with Father. The next time I looked out, Timmy was gone.

"Back to his hood buddies," I muttered. I was afraid he would go even more berserk than he already had, but Mother's death seemed to reach a place inside him that nothing else could.

The next day, he sat down to breakfast with us. His eyes were swollen and red.

"Good morning, Timmy," I said, startled to see him.

"Want a sinker?" he asked, shoving a plate of doughnuts in front of us.

I took one, dipped it into my coffee, and smiled at him.

Timmy kept his eyes down. "I almost went crazy when Robert died. Mother . . . How could she leave us now?"

Father put his hand on Timmy's shoulder and squeezed, then left the mess hall.

"I suppose he's sore at me," Timmy said.

"No, Timmy." I sat across from him and put my hands close to his. "Father's lost right now. Mother was his other half." I broke into tears.

"I'm lost too," Timmy whispered.

"I'd sure like to have my brother back." I wiped my eyes.

Timmy grabbed my hand.

I started seeing changes in Timmy after that day. He joined us for meals and came home before we went to bed.

One night, I saw a shooting star. "Hurry, make a wish," I pointed.

Timmy grinned. "Should it be our old wishes?"

"I haven't thought about them for ages."

"I don't know where I belong. What I'm supposed to do," Timmy said quietly. "Do you think John would let me write to him again?"

Dear Diary,

Audrey is so confused. She doesn't understand where her Grammie went. Why she can't come back and play games with her. She has lost so many loved ones already in her young life. But she's strong. She'll be a survivor.

Timmy is slowly weaning himself from the gangs. I haven't pushed the topic. When he wants to talk, we talk. But I let him bring it up. I'll never have the old Timmy back, but I'd like to have Timmy. Father is deep in mourning. He and Mother were never demonstrative with their love, but they loved intensely. If it weren't for Timmy, I think Father might just have died that day with Mother.

After a couple of weeks, my father and I talked.

"Father, John has asked me to marry him, when the war is over. Do you approve?" My heart pounded. I was sure Father could hear it.

Father nodded tiredly. "John Wilson is the man for you."

"Can I do anything for you?"

"No. I must carry on for my family. You are a grown woman. But Timmy needs a parent. I must be that parent for him."

"I'm not going to abandon you," I said. "We're family."

Father kissed me, then went to bed. He looked so frail. He had lost as many people as I had.

"Please don't fail me," I said to the sky. If there was a God, perhaps he'd listen.

CHAPTER 31
It's Over

On December 17, 1944, Public Proclamation No. 21 was issued, allowing evacuees to return home and lifting contraband regulations. The emotions in Poston ranged from skepticism to guarded hope. I'd believe we were being released when I walked out the front gate.

"When can we leave?" Father asked.

"It's not effective until January 2, 1945," I said.

"Will they just let everyone go?" Father looked small and cautiously hopeful.

"We have to have a destination." I was now the head of our household.

Father, Timmy, Audrey, and I waited another month, until February, before we could leave the camp. I arranged for us to go to Uncle Toshio's.

"It will only be for a short while," I said. "Until we can settle ourselves."

"Won't we go home?" Father asked.

"We have no home to go to, Father."

"The Wilsons will sell our home back to us."

I put my hand on Father's shoulder. "Father, the Wilsons told me the Japanese that returned to California have been

177

chased away. Homes have been burned. Property has been vandalized or stolen. Some people have even been murdered."

"I will never see my orchard again." Father clasped his hands, closing his eyes.

"The Wilsons will sell the house for us. They'll get a better price than we could. We aren't welcomed at home." I held my father's hands as he nodded. "Let the Wilsons do this for us, Father. It's all they can do to try to help us."

"I trust your decision."

Dear Diary,

I know how Father feels. I will never see my home again. Maybe it's best we can't return. I'm afraid we'd be disappointed. Not only in how different things are from our memories of them, but in the atmosphere of our once cozy town. We are hated, simply because of our skin color and our name.

I handed out the last camp paper in January.

We have spent two and a half years in this internment camp. Were we locked away for the protection of the country? Or to prove a point that freedom depends on a person's ancestral makeup?

I have changed deeply during the last three years, as my family also has changed. Several of my family have died, all as a result of this World War. Am I bitter? Yes. My family is smaller than when we came to the camps. But we are strong, and those of us left are hanging together.

But what of those internees who have no family left? What happens now to the oldest generation, whose sons and daughters have died during the war? Those who have no families to return to, because entire families were put behind barbed wire? Those who have no money or home? What do they do now that the government is releasing us? Where do they go?

It's a pity that so many lives have been destroyed for a hateful, prejudiced reason.

As I gathered up our belongings on the day we were scheduled to leave, I noticed some of the older internees sitting huddled together near their barracks.

"Mrs. Abe," I said, gently touching her shoulder. "Aren't you ready to go?"

She looked at me, terror in her eyes. "Where can I go? My family is all gone. I have no one to care for me now."

Mr. Shin nodded. "I will not leave this place. What is left for me out there?"

"You can't stay," I said. "They're closing the camp."

Mrs. Noda shook her head. "We have grown used to the fence."

"There's a large Japanese population in Colorado," I said. "Go there."

"We have no one to go to. You are young. You will take care of your father?"

"Certainly," I said.

"That is how family should be," Mrs. Noda sobbed. "My son will not take me."

"Won't you come to Colorado?" I knelt beside her.

"We are old. What can we offer to Colorado?"

"You offer you!" I cried. "Experiences. Life." I scribbled on some paper. "This is my uncle's address."

The older ones hung their heads. I trudged away, feeling more anger than ever. When I checked later, Mr. Shin had died, sitting in his room. He had been determined not to leave the camp to whatever horrors awaited him outside the fence. I returned to our barracks, surprisingly choked up at leaving the cramped space.

Nancy stood in the doorway, holding Joshua's hand. She looked absolutely wretched. Her hair was oily and snarled. The black circles under her eyes told me she wasn't sleeping. At all. Her fragility was accentuated by the baggy dress she wore.

"Nancy, where are you going?"

"We're going back east with my parents. Mother's relatives settled there before the evacuation. Since I can't support myself, I've got to go where my parents go."

"You've been my best friend since we were four, doll."

"I'm going to miss you, Margaret Yamaguchi."

"You too, Nancy Yamaguchi. But you have to visit. So we can see Joshua." I hugged Nancy; I couldn't reach her anymore. "Here's Uncle Toshio's address. Write me when you get settled, so we can make arrangements to meet."

"It's not the same as living across the street," Nancy said as I picked up Joshua.

"Do you think you'll stay there?" I felt tears coming and didn't try to stop them.

"I have to finish high school now. Mother agreed to watch Joshua."

I squeezed Joshua tight and pecked him goodbye.

"I've got to pack, lamb pie." Nancy stuck an address in my hand, scooped Joshua up, and hurried away. She looked much older than she had a few months ago. Robert's death had almost killed her.

"I love you both!" I called as Nancy ran to her room. Would I see her again? I suspected my family was a painful reminder of Robert. I grabbed Audrey and hugged her tight. My tears turned to sobs, so Audrey patted my face.

Later that day, Father and I toted our meager bundles to the gate.

"Margaret, I am proud of you," Father said.

"For what?" I asked.

"You have conducted yourself as a lady in the camp. You have held our battered family together, especially after the deaths we have suffered. You took care of your niece as your daughter. You will be fine on your own."

"It will be a long time before I'm on my own, Father." I touched his cheek.

Father nodded, then returned to our room. Did he think I could just walk away from him once we left the camp? I strolled through the camp once more, and ran into Sharon Ito in the mess hall.

"Margaret, I've been looking for you. I wanted to say goodbye. And thanks."

I hugged Sharon. "Thanks for what?"

"For being my friend. You helped me see how important following a dream is."

"What do you mean?" I asked.

"I'm going to get a degree in art. If I can survive this camp, I can do anything," Sharon said. "You gave me a chance to use my art."

Father, Timmy, Audrey, and I boarded the bus to take us away from the camp. As I stepped outside the fence for the first time since we had arrived, I breathed in the air. It seemed cleaner. I was free! I didn't want to be cooped up or restrained again.

CHAPTER 32
Starting Over

Father, Timmy, Audrey, and I arrived in Denver on February 4, 1945. Uncle Toshio, Aunt Aiko, Steven, and Dorothy waited at the terminal. I couldn't bear to be on the bus another moment. I felt as if the air was being sucked out of the cabin. I grabbed Audrey and stumbled for the door. As I stepped onto the sidewalk, I breathed my first free breath in almost three years. Several other families had also traveled to Denver. Sadly, none of the elderly had followed.

Dorothy looked super in her freshly pressed clothes. She was wearing a full skirt, new shoes, and white bobby socks.

"I must look a mess." I smoothed my mended dress, feeling old and frumpy.

"You look wonderful," Uncle Toshio said. "We are pleased you will live with us."

"Grammie!" Audrey cried, reaching for Aunt Aiko, who snatched Audrey up and cradled her. She cooed and sang to Audrey, who clapped her hands delightedly.

"What's the first thing you want to do?" Dorothy asked.

"Take a bath," I said. "A long, hot bubble bath, in private."

"We can arrange that!" Dorothy burst. She hooked her arm through mine and sauntered to the car. Steven carried bags.

As Uncle Toshio drove, I relaxed and stared out the window. The winter sunshine was bright and filled my world with a warm glow. There was snow on the ground, and I was chilly, but I was out of Poston. Father and I had no money, no home, and no jobs. But we had family. Many internees didn't. Entire families had been imprisoned in the camps and had no one to help them get on their feet. Maybe it was a blessing after all that Uncle Toshio left before the evacuation.

"It's amazing!" I said. "I've forgotten how lovely a city can be."

Dorothy held my hand. "It's divine, isn't it? I'll show you all around."

There were crowds of people walking on the sidewalks. Cars were zipping up and down the streets. Everywhere I looked, I saw different kinds of faces.

"Does Denver have a diversified population?" I asked.

"Yes," Dorothy answered. "There are all kinds of people."

Uncle Toshio parked in front of a modest home in a well-kept neighborhood.

"You'll room with me," Dorothy said, grabbing my bag.

"Audrey needs to sleep with me," I said.

"There are two beds in my room. It'll be like a sleep over."

I walked into the house, sank onto the floor in the hallway, and sobbed. "Thank you for opening your home to us. I don't know what we would have done."

"This is your home, too," Uncle Toshio said and helped me up. "I only wish we could have done something during your time in the camp."

Steven dragged Timmy to the basement, where they would share a room. I heard them wrestling.

After a huge lunch, Father and Uncle Toshio discussed the future.

"Will you stay here, with us?" Uncle Toshio asked.

"Only until we can support ourselves," Father said proudly. Father looked much older than Toshio, even though Toshio was the older brother. It hadn't struck me until that moment how much my father had aged in the camp. How much of his life he had lost. And yet, he felt no bitterness toward the American government. He still viewed the internment as a huge mistake. I couldn't accept that. My high school years, my first love, had been ripped away from me. I couldn't get that back. Money and homes could be rebuilt. Not my childhood.

"You are my brother, my family," Toshio said. "My home is your home. But I was speaking more of a work venture."

"I see," said my father. "Like what?"

"An orchard cannot grow in this part of the nation, but we *can* work the earth."

"I am listening." Father's eyes seemed to brighten a bit.

"There is a smaller town near here, where the dirt would be good for row crop farming. I have saved my money since we moved here and have enough for a down payment on an acreage. Would you be interested?"

"I have no money," Father said.

I interrupted. "Father, the Wilsons are selling our house. What about that?"

"We need a new house, Margaret."

"What if we pool our money, purchase our land and build ourselves a large house where everyone can live?" Uncle Toshio said.

"Is there enough?" Father asked.

"I believe there will be. It will take hard work, but we are used to that."

"What do you think, Margaret?"

"I think it's a perfect plan."

For the first time in months, my father's eyes sparkled. I scanned the classified ads as my father and uncle talked more. I had to raise tuition money if I wanted to attend college in the fall. How I wanted to! But what could I do? How could I compete with people who had been working while I was locked in an internment camp? What work skills *did* I have? I shook those thoughts to the back of my mind. I circled three jobs that sounded promising.

"Margaret," Dorothy said. "Let's go shopping. You need a new dress."

"I will look after the darling," Aunt Aiko volunteered.

"I don't have any money," I admitted.

"I've saved some from my secretary's job."

I felt more tears coming. "I'll pay you back after I get a job." New clothes. It had been so long since I had worn anything new.

"No," Dorothy insisted. "This is my gift." She pulled me outside. "I wasn't very nice when you and John first dated. I feel like a drone."

"But you don't have to," I started.

"Let me do this for you, okay?"

I took a quick bath and borrowed a dress from Dorothy. I had lost so much weight in the camp, it was a little big. But I felt like a different person with a pretty dress on.

Dorothy and I went downtown after lunch. I had a hard time walking around Denver. I expected someone to shout at me and tell me to get back behind the fence. But no one did. I felt awkward and conspicuous.

"The new fashions are so fun," I said, smoothing the type of skirt Dorothy wore.

"It's called the bobby soxer," Dorothy explained. "It's more casual than you'll want for a job. More for dates and school."

The colors and fabrics I saw in the stores thrilled me. "These are gorgeous!"

"Why don't we get you one ready-made outfit, then look through the patterns?" Dorothy helped me choose a neutral color for the ready-made dress, shoes, and a hat. Then we selected a pattern and found some fabric on sale. "We'll get our hair done."

"It's been so long since I had a shampoo," I said.

Dorothy pulled my hand. "I've been waiting a long time to splurge on you."

"I can't thank you enough," I said.

"I can't imagine how icky it was for you in the camp. This can't possibly make up for three years of your life."

After my hair was styled, I looked in the mirror. A different face stared back at me. I felt almost dilly with all the fuss. I touched my hair and smiled. "My hair hasn't been this shiny for a long time."

Dorothy put her face next to mine and looked into the mirror. The differences between us couldn't be seen. But I felt them. Did everyone around me know I had been in the camp?

"We could stare at ourselves all day," Dorothy said. "Let's go to the campus." Dorothy and I picked up college catalogs, then planned my job-hunting strategy.

"I got my job through my college advisor," Dorothy said. "I'll see if I can come up with something. What do you like to do?"

"I like to write. I'm pretty good at it," I gushed. "I've been taking secretarial courses and know the basics."

When we arrived home, Aunt Aiko was fussing over Audrey. "It is nice to have a little one in the house again. She has Barbara's eyes."

I picked up Audrey. "I can't imagine not having her in my life."

"You are a good mother. You look lovely." Aunt Aiko ushered me into a chair and fed me milk and cookies. Even though I felt silly, at my age, eating a child's snack, I liked the feeling of being fussed over.

Aunt Aiko was different from Mother. She was plumper, but very nurturing. She wasn't as quiet as Mother had been, and was easy to talk to. After I finished the cookies, I laughed and hugged her. Then I cried. "Thank you," I kept sobbing.

Aunt Aiko held me until I was drained.

"Let me help you with dinner." I wiped my eyes.

"Not tonight," Aunt Aiko said sternly. "Go upstairs and settle into your room."

I climbed the stairs with Audrey, then grabbed my pen.

Dear Diary,

I feel good about coming to Colorado. There is a large Japanese population, and I don't feel the animosity that I felt in California. Mostly, though, I'm with family again. I had taken my family for granted when we lived in Valle Verde. I will never do that again. Audrey seems to be adjusting to her new family. Aunt Aiko doesn't mind being Grammie. Timmy and Steven are getting along well. It's good for Timmy to have someone older again. Maybe it will help him get straightened out. And, thank the Lord, Father is accepting Uncle Toshio's generous help. I worried about Father's being too proud to stay here. It's good for him to be near his brother again.

He will heal; we all will, with enough time. Uncle Toshio is enjoying being the elder man in the family. I think he feels incredible guilt over our stay in the internment camp. I can forgive him and forgive Father now. My heart has suffered enough hurt, and I have survived enough horror that I can't retain a grudge. Both men did what they thought was best.

The next day, Dorothy called from work. "Can you go to a job interview at ten o'clock? An advertising agency needs a secretary right away."

Despite my lack of experience, the agency gave me a chance. "I like your style," Mr. Atkinson said. "You're a sharp cookie."

Starting the following day, I would be earning a paycheck. My aunt agreed to watch Audrey. Father decided to wait until fall to enroll Timmy into school.

"It is hard enough adjusting to new surroundings. He will wait until next school year, then enter the appropriate grade."

Since he was fourteen, Timmy worked around the house. He shoveled snow in the neighborhood, ran odd jobs for the man in the hardware store, and delivered papers. In his spare time, Timmy studied.

"I barely did any work in the camps," he admitted. "The teachers didn't really care if we learned anything."

"Want some tutoring?" Steven offered. "I'm going to be a teacher. If I can help a bird like Timmy, I'll be able to teach anyone."

Timmy grinned.

Uncle Toshio found Father a job in the factory where he worked. They agreed to look into the farming venture. "I think the soil is good for onions," Uncle Toshio said.

"It has been too long since I worked in good soil," Father sifted through the dirt.

By the end of March, the Wilsons had sold our house and wired the money to Father. The government had seized the orchard property when we were evacuated, so my father and uncle got no money out of it. Besides losing millions of dollars in revenue, they lost the land they had lovingly worked for so many years. The Wilsons sent their regrets. They hadn't sold the car yet.

Dear Diary,

I'm working hard at my job, saving every penny. Everyone in our house works, and I'm grateful. I see many Japanese Americans who are homeless and jobless. I found out today about camp friends who are starving because they couldn't get work.

One day, I found a letter from Sharon in the mail.

Dear Margaret,

Can you believe we both ended up in Denver? Let's meet some Saturday for lunch and shopping. I'm working part-time at the daily newspaper. Just running copy, but I'm learning the business. I'm anxious for college. The future looks good .

Did John and I have a future together?

CHAPTER 33
Goodbyes

"What's wrong, Father?" I asked.

"I miss my wife."

"Why don't we plant a memory garden when we build the house?"

"I will have a spot to sit with her."

After Father received the money from the Wilsons, he and Uncle Toshio put a down payment on a chunk of land.

Dear Diary,

As winter turns to spring, everyone's spirit seems to improve. The war continues, but we seem distant from it. I've received only one letter from Nancy. We've shared so much pain, perhaps it's best we lose touch with one another. After all, we've been drifting apart for three years. I know my father misses Joshua. I miss Joshua. He's the only link to Robert we have left. I'm angry at Nancy for keeping him from us. We went from seeing him daily to nothing. Audrey can't understand why he can't play with her.

My job was better than I could have dreamed. The agency owner looked at some of my essays and gave me some clients. Within two months, I was a copywriter. By the middle of summer,

I had saved enough to pay for my tuition, so I enrolled for the fall session at the University of Colorado. My employer was lenient about my schedule. As long as I completed my work, I could do it any time.

> *Dear Diary,*
>
> *I worry about John all the time. But somehow, being out of the camp, I don't dwell on the negative so much. I write him every day. I keep him informed on Audrey and send him pictures.*
>
> *He calls her his little girl.*
>
> *Timmy is going like gangbusters with Steven's tutoring. He's stopped smoking, and he and Father are getting along better.*

By July, the heat and humidity were unbearable. So was the news we received from New York. Mrs. Sato wrote us a note:

> *Dear friends,*
>
> *I have bad news. Our Nancy could not cope with so much sadness and loss from the war. We thought once we left the camp, she would be better. She was not. She was ashamed of being in Poston and stayed in the house day and night. She refused to bathe or eat or take care of Joshua. Nancy took her life last week. I am sorry to ask, but could you take little Joshua? My husband is in poor health, and I simply cannot take care of them both. This is a burden, I realize, but I have no choice.*

I read the letter, sobbing, to my father. "We can't let Joshua go."

"He belongs with us." For the first time since Mother died, Father sounded sure of his words. "A child is not a burden."

I called Mrs. Sato. "We'll come for Joshua on the train."

Father smiled as I hung up the phone.

I wiped my eyes. "I'll take him, as I took Audrey."

"That is much for one so young." Father looked at me and took my hand. "What if your John does not return? Could you take two children alone?"

"I have faith John will return, Father." I wasn't angry with him or hurt by what he said. "If John doesn't come home, I'll raise these children as my own."

Father embraced me, and we cried together. It felt good to let the tears out. And I was relieved my father was feeling more emotion.

The day after we arrived home with Joshua, the paper read:

JAPAN SURRENDERS. WAR IS OVER.

"The war is over?" I said. "Just like that, and the war is over." I thought of Robert and Howard. Mother, Barbara, and Nancy were casualties as much as if they had been on the front. Five people I loved had died. And now, five words in the paper announced the end of a horrible war.

I read the report in the paper. The United States had dropped a nuclear bomb on the city of Hiroshima. I was sick to my stomach and torn. Relief swept through me because the war was over. But anguish was written on my father's face.

The bomb caused such devastation to the city that Father's family was probably gone. I squeezed his hand; he simply nodded, accepting this fact as he had accepted everything else over the last three years.

The destruction of Hiroshima and Nagasaki ended World War II. Joshua blended into our family. Audrey was thrilled to see her cousin. And the two of them helped all of us find joy and deal with our new lives. But my life was still incomplete. I had heard nothing from John for weeks.

Two weeks after the bombing, Mrs. Wilson called. "Margaret, John's coming home."

"Do you know when to expect him?"

"Soon."

I hoped he'd make it home before school started. Did he expect me to return to California? It was September before Mrs. Wilson called again. "They're shipping him home next week, honey. He'll be within hugging distance soon."

I was on pins and needles all the time. I wanted to run all the way to California to meet his train.

The next week, the phone rang. "Hello," my father answered. "Yes." He handed the phone to me with a shrug.

"Hello?" I said.

"Hi, beautiful."

"John!" I screamed. My legs gave out, and I sunk to my knees.

"I just got home today."

Tears burst out of my eyes. "When can I see you?"

"As soon as I can get to Denver."

"Can we pick you up at the train?"

"No. I'll be out there by the end of the week. Margaret?"

"Yes," I whispered.

"I love you."

Friday evening, as I returned home from work, I saw Father's old car in our driveway. Sitting on our porch were Uncle Toshio, Aunt Aiko, Father, Timmy, and John, holding Audrey and Joshua on his lap. His face looked fuller. His hair was buzzed. He seemed bigger than I remembered. I was strangely nervous and paused. I stared at a stranger. He turned his head.

Once I saw his eyes and his smile, I knew he was my John. My fear melted away. I ran to him. I jumped into his arms and grabbed him as hard as possible. I sobbed into his shoulder. I could feel him, smell him, and taste him. I didn't want to let go. He put me on the ground and kissed me, long and hard. I grabbed him tighter. I couldn't speak but gazed at his face.

"My pearl." John held my hands, and a tear ran down his cheek. "I didn't know if I'd ever see you again."

I cried wet, gigantic tears. Relief flooded over me as John kissed those tears away.

As I said goodbye to the camps and the life I had before that, I said hello to another one. My real life. With John.

APPENDIX
The Bitter Truth

During World War II, only 10 people were convicted of spying for the empire of Japan. All 10 were Caucasian.

Almost 120,000 Japanese Americans along the West Coast were forcibly relocated to internment camps following the attack on Pearl Harbor. Their only crime was having Japanese ancestry.

Two-thirds of the 120,000 people who were forcibly relocated were American citizens, having been born in the United States.

The 442nd Regimental Combat Team, consisting of all-Nisei soldiers, is recognized as the most decorated unit in U.S. history. They earned a total of 18,000 awards, including 9,500 Purple Hearts and 52 Distinguished Service Crosses.

Despite promises from the government, property owned by Japanese Americans before the internment was permanently transferred to Caucasians. In effect, those interned had their property, their bank accounts, and their houses stolen by people who assured them that everything would be returned at the end of the war.

In 1982, 37 years after the end of World War II, the Commission of Wartime Relocation and Internment of Civilians determined that the internment was "motivated largely by racial prejudice and wartime hysteria."

In 1988, every former internee received a $20,000 reparation and an apology from the government. For most, the apology was more important than the money.

FOR FURTHER READING

Chan, Sucheng. *Asian Americans: An Interpretive History.* Boston: Twayne, 1991.

Daniels, Roger, and Eric Foner, eds. *Prisoners without Trial: Japanese Americans in World War II.* New York: Hill and Wang, 1993.

Fremon, David K. *Japanese American Internment in American History.* Springfield, N.J.: Enslow Publishers, 1996.

Houston, Jeanne Wakatsaki, and James D. Houston. *Farewell to Manzanar: A True Story of Japanese American Experience during and after World War II Internment.* San Francisco: Bantam, 1974.

Stanley, Jerry. *I Am an American: A True Story of the Japanese Internment.* New York: Crown Publishers, 1994.

Takaki, Ronald. *Strangers from a Different Shore: History of Asian Americans.* Little, Brown, and Co., 1989. Reprint, Back Bay Books, 1998.

Web sites

The Japanese American Internment : www.oz.net/~cyu/intern-ment/main.html

An excellent source of materials for anyone interested in this topic, this site contains historical information leading up to the war, a glossary, and time line, information about camp life, and many photographs. Highly recommended!

Japanese American Relocation Collection, University of Utah: www.lib.utah.edu

Japanese American National Museum (Los Angeles): www.janm.org

Museum of the City of San Francisco: www.sfmuseum.org

This site has numerous photographs pertaining to the internment, including those of Dorothea Lange.

National Archives and Records Administration: www.nara.gov

President Roosevelt's radio address following the Pearl Harbor attack is available at this site. FDR's actual notes can be viewed. His address to Congress, requesting that the United States declare war, is also available.

Newspaper headlines and clippings from throughout the war can be looked up.

War Relocation Authority Camps in Arizona, 1942–1946, University of Arizona Library: www.library.arizona.edu

Extensive information about all aspects of camp life, including photographs and maps, is included in this web site.